Cody Havlicek, Texas Ranger, is a moral man. He is totally dedicated to enforcing the law and will do whatever it takes to bring wrongdoers to justice.

When a series of murders, including that of a fellow Ranger, takes place in the Big Bend region, he is ordered to track down the men responsible. Cody and a young boy he rescued must face and defeat the diabolical criminals. The twisted confrontations and nearly insurmountable hardships along the way cause Cody to doubt his own abilities. He must oppose single-handedly a large group of criminals and find the strength needed to bring the killers to justice.

Big Bend Death Trap is not so much a traditional Western as it is a mystery with a Western setting. As Cody will find out, the roots of the crimes he is investigating reach all the way back to the state capital in Austin, where the treachery of one man leaves the young Ranger literally on the brink of death.

Big Bend Death Trap
is exciting reading for nearly all ages.

BIG BEND DEATH TRAP

OTHER TEXAS RANGER NOVELS

By
James J. Griffin

TROUBLE RIDES THE TEXAS PACIFIC

BORDER RAIDERS

TRAIL OF THE RENEGADE

RANGER JUSTICE

PANHANDLE RAIDERS

BIG BEND DEATH TRAP

A TEXAS RANGER CODY HAVLICEK STORY

James J. Griffin

James J. Griffin

Condor Publishing, Inc.
Lincoln, Michigan

BIG BEND DEATH TRAP
A Texas Ranger Cody Havlicek Story

September 2007

*Cover illustration: Gail Heath, Harrisville, Michigan

*Texas Ranger badge image provided as a courtesy by the
 Texas Ranger Hall of Fame and Museum of Waco, Texas

ISBN 978-1-931079-05-1

CONDOR PUBLISHING, INC.
PO Box 39
123 S. Barlow Road
Lincoln, MI 48742-0039
WWW.CONDORPUBLISHINGINC.COM

Printed in the United States of America

In memory of my mother Ruth, for my father Willis,

sisters Beverly and Ruth, and brother William.

1

Texas Ranger Cody Havlicek stood slightly crouched; his left hand hovered over the gun on his hip as he gazed at the gunman facing him. The young killer's eyes seemed a reflection of Cody's own clear blue ones.

"Now, Ranger!" the gunman challenged.

Cody's hand slashed downward for his gun and lifted it cleanly from its holster. The youthful gunman was lightning fast as he drew his pistol, aimed at the Ranger's belt buckle, and fired twice. Cody clutched at his middle, jackknifed, and fell to the dirt. He lay writhing in agony.

"I said ya weren't fast enough to beat me," the renegade sneered as he stood over the downed Ranger. "Plugged ya right in the belly."

"Ya got me all right, ya no-good...lowdown...gut-shootin'...sidewinder. I'm done for."

The Ranger's voice trailed off. Cody gasped as he clamped both hands to his middle once again while his body shuddered and went slack.

"CODY! ANDY!"

"And your mom's gonna kill both of us," Cody chuckled, "if we don't get back for supper."

The lanky Ranger pushed himself to his feet and grinned at the gunman, Andy, his seven year old son. Cody tousled the boy's shock of blonde hair.

"Nice shootin'," he praised the boy. "You're gonna make a fine

Ranger one day. Bet a hat on it."

Cody passed the wooden six-gun back to his son and replaced it with his own Colt Peacemaker.

Cody's wife, Sarah, waited for them on the porch of their neat, whitewashed ranch house. Her hazel eyes flared with mock indignation as they approached.

"Cody, I told you to fetch Andy for supper, not disappear on me. And just look at the two of you all covered in dirt. I swear, you're more of a little boy than Andy. You'll have to clean up before I let you into my kitchen. I just scrubbed the floor. And be quiet; I finally got Abigail to sleep."

"Yes, ma'am," Cody replied, favoring her with one of his crooked smiles.

"C'mon, Andy, let's wash up."

Father and son headed for the pump behind the house.

Sarah watched out the back door as Cody and Andy ducked their heads into the trough. She smiled as the boy mimicked his dad's every move. Andy worshipped his lawman father. Her anger faded. . .until she saw a shadow at the side window. Sarah shouted furiously, grabbed a broom, and raced outside.

"CODY THOMAS HAVLICEK! Your pie-biter horse is at it again!"

"Uh-oh, Dad. Yank's gonna get you in trouble," Andy said.

Cody's big chestnut paint gelding raced for the safety of the barn.

"I'd better go rescue him from your Mom," Cody chuckled as he draped a towel around his shoulders.

Yankee was a one-man animal whose vicious teeth and hooves had done in more than one lawbreaker. The powerfully built horse was afraid of no one except Sarah.

"Andy, you finish washin' up, then head inside and keep an eye on your sister," his father ordered.

Cody entered the barn and laughed. Yankee snorted in his stall while Sarah threatened to hit him with her broom. Sizzle, Andy's pet sorrel paint gelding, stood nervously stamping in his own stall.

"It's not funny, Cody. You let him out again," Sarah scolded.

"I swear I didn't, honey," Cody protested. "He was in the corral.

He must've opened the gate."

Cody slid by his wife to rub Yankee's velvety muzzle. The horse whickered.

"Don't blame me that there isn't any apple pie with supper. That biscuit-eater of yours just stole it from the windowsill."

Sarah glared at them. Yankee did his best to hide behind Cody.

"I don't know why I bother," Sarah sighed in frustration. "You let that horse do whatever he wants."

"I let you do whatever you want also, darlin'," Cody soothed, taking her in his arms.

"Cody, don't you try and get out of this," Sarah warned, her resolve fading as he kissed her.

She ran her fingers through his thick blonde hair. Her husband's lips pressed harder as she tried to push him away.

"Oh, go on with you, Cody. Supper's already on the table. Finish washing up before it gets cold."

With a slight smile, she headed for the house.

"Thanks, Yank. That was better'n any apple pie," Cody told his horse as he closed the stall door.

*   *   *

"We always say grace before we eat," Cody reminded Andy as the boy reached across the table for a warm biscuit.

Behind her brother's chair, Abigail, Andy's infant sister, slept in her cradle.

"Sorry, Dad," Andy apologized.

"It's all right. You lead us, son."

"Sure, Dad," the boy answered. He closed his eyes and prayed, *"Bless us, O Lord, and these thy gifts which we are about to receive from thy bounty, through Christ our Lord. Amen."*

Sarah dished out chicken and potatoes and the family started to eat. Cody stopped to listen, then put down his fork. Hoofbeats drifted on the still air.

"Rider comin'," he observed. "Best see who it is."

Cody pushed back from the table, loosened his Colt in its holster, and headed out onto the porch.

"Howdy, Cody," greeted Ranger Jace Morgan as he reined his horse to a halt. "I reckon you know why I'm here."

"Yep, suppose I do," Cody answered the rookie.

Sarah and Andy stepped out onto the porch. The young Ranger touched the brim of his hat in a polite greeting.

"Miz Havlicek...Andy."

"Cap'n Blawcyzk have orders for me?" asked Cody.

"He sure does," Jace replied. "He said you can spend tonight at home, but he wants to see you first thing in the mornin'."

"Tell him I'll be at Headquarters bright and early."

"Jace, would you like to join us for supper?" Sarah asked. "There's still plenty of chicken and bisquits left. I can't offer you any apple pie, though. Cody's horse stole it."

"I'd purely admire some, ma'am," Jace drawled. "But the Cap'n wanted me to head straight back as soon as I found Cody." The young Ranger chuckled as he added, "And I sure wouldn't fight Yankee for a piece of that pie."

The horse's bad temper was well-known by all of the Rangers.

"I don't care what Captain Blawcyzk says," Sarah insisted. "You can at least take a few minutes while I wrap up some chicken and bisquits for you to eat on the way back. You wait right there while I fetch it."

"Yes, ma'am," Jace agreed while his gelding fidgeted under him. Sarah headed into the kitchen.

"Sorry I had to bring you word from the Cap'n so quick, Cody. I know you've only been home a few days."

"That's not your fault, Jace. I've been expectin' this. You gonna be ridin' with me?"

"Don't reckon so. The Cap'n said somethin' about me and a couple of the other boys headin' down to Laredo and joinin' up with Company D."

"Bet you're gonna chase a bunch of Comanches," Andy excitedly broke in.

"Can't say as to that, Andy." Jace couldn't help but grin at the youngster's enthusiasm. "But I'll wager there'll be some shootin' involved."

"There usually is," Cody sighed. "Mebbe someday we'll be able to hang up our guns for good."

"Not until Texas settles down, I'm afraid," Jace answered as Sarah stepped back onto the porch.

"Here's your chicken and biscuits," she smiled. "I hope that's enough for you."

"Thank you, ma'am. I reckon I'd better be ridin'. The Cap'n don't like to be kept waitin'."

"You be careful, Jace," Cody warned.

"You do the same," Jace replied. "*Adios!*"

He heeled his horse into a lope.

*   *   *

Cody and his family lingered over supper for quite some time. Once the dishes had been put away, man and wife sat in the porch swing and watched the sunset. Andy chased lizards around the yard while Abigail slept peacefully in a wicker basket. Sarah snuggled against Cody and rested her head on his chest. Twilight slowly descended.

"I'd hoped we'd have a few more days together," she whispered.

"Maybe next time," Cody replied. "You…"

"Shhh, I know," Sarah said softly. "You can't ever stay in one place for long. I knew that when I married you. It didn't stop me."

"You could've done a lot better'n marryin' a tumbleweedin' Texas Ranger."

"But I love that tumbleweed Ranger," Sarah replied. "And I always will." She sighed deeply. "We'd better head inside. You'll want to get a good night's rest before riding out."

"In a little while," Cody replied, pulling her closer.

They remained on the porch, wrapped in each other's arms, until the cooling night air sent them back inside for one last night together.

"Cody," she questioned as they lay side by side in the dark. "Do you ever wish you were still single?"

"Sarah, what kind of silly question is that?"

"There are lots of pretty girls out there that you must run across all the time."

"I'm not interested in any of the women I meet, no matter how good lookin' they might be. You're the handsomest woman in Texas. I love you, Sarah, and I married you. You're the only woman I'll ever want."

"Are you sure, Cody?" Sarah persisted.

"I'm absolutely positive," Cody assured her. "Look what you do for me. You put up with my gallivantin' all over Texas, never knowin' when I'll come home. You're a great cook, a wonderful lover, and you run the ranch while I'm gone. You gave me Andy and Abby. Heck, you even put up with Yankee. What more could a man want?"

"Do you really mean that?"

"I guess I'll just have to prove it to you."

*   *   *

Cody rose well before sunrise. While he packed his saddlebags, Sarah cooked a huge breakfast. Once the meal was finished, Cody and Andy headed for the barn to saddle Yankee. The big paint whickered his eagerness to be on the trail. Cody entered his stall and slipped the horse a peppermint candy.

"Take it easy, bud," Cody chided. "We'll be ridin' for quite a spell, I'd imagine. You'll have plenty of time to stretch your legs."

Yankee nuzzled his rider's shoulder. Cody took the saddle and blanket off the rail and placed them on the gelding's broad back.

The Ranger stood in the front yard, reins in hand, ready to travel. He took Abigail from her mother's arms and let the baby snuggle against his chest. The infant gurgled happily and Cody kissed her on the forehead. Reluctantly, he handed her back to Sarah.

"Andy, you take care of your mom, and do your chores. Make sure to help her with your sister. And don't forget catechism."

Cody tousled his son's hair.

"Sure, Dad."

Cody turned back to Sarah.

"Honey, I'll be back soon's I can. Cap'n Blawcyzk will let you know I'm okay."

"Please be careful, Cody."

Sarah shifted her gaze to Yankee.

"You're forgiven, Yank," she assured the paint. "Just bring Cody back home, and I'll bake you the biggest apple pie you've ever seen."

She patted his shoulder and the big horse nickered.

Cody enfolded Sarah in his arms and kissed her tenderly.

"I love you so much," he whispered.

"And I love you. All I ask is that you come home in one piece."

"I promise you that."

Cody kissed his wife once again and swung into the saddle.

"Let's go, Yank."

He heeled the gelding into a lope.

2

Cody draped Yankee's reins over the tooth-marked hitchrail in front of Ranger Headquarters in Austin. Captain James Blawcyzk was waiting for him when he stepped into the captain's cramped office. Blawcyzk greeted him with a broad smile.

"Howdy, Cody. Glad you got here so quickly. Have a seat."

"Buda's not that far from Austin," Cody responded.

Both men were originally from Bandera, a small cattle town northwest of San Antonio. It was one of the first Polish settlements in the United States. Blawcyzk's family had been among the original settlers of the town. Cody had come to Texas from New Hampshire to join relatives in the Lone Star State. Blawcyzk himself had recruited Havlicek, his distant cousin.

Cody took a chair in the corner, hooking his bootheels over a rung. Blawcyzk limped over to a file cabinet and removed a thick manila folder. He settled into a battered chair behind a scarred desk.

"Leg botherin' you much, Cap'n?" Cody inquired.

Blawcyzk grimaced when he straightened his left leg to slide it under the desk.

"More some days than others," Blawcyzk shrugged. "Today's one of the bad ones. There must be a storm rollin' in."

Jim Blawcyzk was only a few years older than Cody. Earlier in his career, Blawcyzk fought it out with three killers in San Angelo. The renegades died with Blawcyzk's lead in them but not before they shattered his left leg. It left him a cripple and unable to ride great distances. As the captain at Ranger Headquarters, his years of experience gave invaluable leadership to the men in the field.

"How's your family?" asked Blawcyzk. "The baby all right?"

"They're doin' right well," responded Cody. "Thanks for askin'."

"Glad to hear it," the captain replied.

He took a piece of licorice from a jar on his desk and popped it into his mouth.

"You want one?" Blawcyck asked, shoving the jar across the desk.

"Sure," Cody answered, taking a piece of the candy. "My sweet tooth's almost as bad as yours."

Blawcyzk laughed as he leaned back in his chair.

"I can't argue with you there, but I think your horse has us both beat in that department."

Blawcyzk's expression turned grim as he glanced over the contents of the file he held.

"Let's get down to business. A few weeks back we got a request for help from Mark Carlisle, the sheriff of Brewster County. There's been a couple of killin's down that way, includin' a rancher named Peter Hunt. He owned the biggest spread in the county. It's all in here."

Blawcyzk removed a letter from the file and passed it to Cody.

"Hunt's kin in San Antonio have been makin' a big fuss demandin' his killer be found. They've got a lot of influence here in Austin. They've been puttin' pressure on the Governor and Adjutant General, who in turn have been puttin' pressure on me."

"Killer or killers," Cody replied.

"That's right," the captain agreed.

The wrinkles in Blawcyzk's weathered countenance deepened.

"I sent Chance Lowney down there. As I recollect, you rode with him for a spell."

"I sure did, Cap'n—'bout a year after I signed on with the Rangers. We were saddle pards while we were with Company C out of Del Rio. Chance is one tough hombre. He taught me quite a bit."

Blawcyzk shifted the licorice in his cheek, then continued.

"You've heard of those new-fangled photographs, haven't you? They've been around since before the War, but they're still none too common."

"Yeah, I've seen a few of 'em," Cody replied. "I'd like to get one of Sarah and the kids taken some day. Any particular reason you ask, Cap'n?"

"Two weeks ago, I got this in the mail."

Blawcyzk slid a photograph across his desk. Cody drew his breath in sharply as he stared at its subject—Ranger Chance Lowney, with two bloody bullet holes in his chest, lying dead on a board sidewalk.

"This came with it."

Blawcyzk passed Cody a torn sheet of paper which read: *We don't want any Rangers in Brewster County. Send more, and they'll get the same.*

"That all there was?"

"That's it. The only clue we have as to where that picture was taken is a Marathon postmark. There's no photographer's name, no signature on that note—not that you'd expect one."

Blawcyzk's deep blue eyes flared with anger as he bit off another piece of licorice, then continued.

"After I received that photograph, I sent Hap Tompkins to Marathon. He's a seasoned veteran as tough as they come, but he never made it there. I wired Sheriff Carlisle over at Alpine, but Tompkins never met up with him either. So we've got one Ranger dead, and another missin' and most likely dead."

"And you want me to find their killers."

Cody's voice was low and deadly.

"Along with whoever killed Peter Hunt and those others. I would've liked to send Dade French or Jim Huggins along with you, but they're still on assignment up in the Panhandle. You'll be on your own, Cody."

Cody smiled for a moment at the thought of riding with Dade French or Jim Huggins. French was a wiry young Ranger whose jet black hair and eyes sometimes confused people into thinking him a Mexican or half-breed Indian. French often used his swarthy appearance to play one of those parts, allowing him to work well undercover. On their first assignment together, Cody and Dade had become fast friends. Sergeant Jim Huggins was a tough veteran who'd once saved Cody's life during a battle with renegade Comanches down in the Nueces Strip.

"How's ol' Dade doin'?" Cody asked. "And how about Jim and his boy Dan?"

Huggins' teenaged son, Daniel, had recently signed up with the Rangers.

"They're all doin' fine," Blawcyzk replied. "Dan Huggins is with Company B over Eagle Pass way. He's gonna be a fine Ranger. But enough talk about those men. Are you all right with takin' on this assignment single-handedly?"

"I've been on my own before, Cap'n, and I kind of prefer it that way," Cody truthfully answered. "Besides, one man's less likely to attract notice than two or three."

"I knew you'd see it like that," Blawcyzk grinned.

"You'd better keep your badge in your pocket," the captain advised, with a glance at the silver star on silver circle pinned to Cody's shirt.

While the Rangers wore no uniforms, and most didn't wear a badge, Havlicek, like some others, had hand-carved his own badge from a Mexican ten-peso coin.

"I don't want to see you end up like Chance Lowney. Be careful."

"You can bet a hat on that, Cap'n. Guess I'll be ridin'."

Cody pushed up from the chair and, with a touch of his Stetson brim in a quick salute, turned on his heels and strode out of the office.

Captain Blawcyzk stood at his window watching as Cody unwrapped Yankee's reins from the hitchrail, swung into the saddle, and loped the big paint down Capitol Avenue. The captain limped over to the stove in the corner, lifted the chipped enamel coffeepot from the surface, and removed a mug from the shelf.

"I sure hope I'm not sendin' you on a suicide mission, Cody," he murmured fervently as horse and rider faded from sight.

Blawcyzk poured a full measure of coffee, then downed it. Refilling the mug, he slumped into his chair, absently turning the cup in his hand as he studied the thick black brew.

3

"**G**uess we'd better find a place to spend the night, pardner."

Cody spoke to his horse as the sun descended toward the western horizon and the sky flamed crimson and gold. Yankee nickered. The pair had traveled through the brush choked chaparral country of Southwest Texas. They headed for Alpine, the Brewster County seat. Both man and horse were gaunt and travel-stained. They had been on the trail for a week and still had two more days of hard riding to reach their destination. Here, deep in the badlands of the West Texas plains, waterholes and creeks were few and far between.

Dusk fell and the sky faded from pale blue to indigo. Cody spotted a thin patch of greenery. He pushed his weary mount into a trot and reined in alongside a small *cienega*. As the Ranger climbed out of the saddle, the paint snorted his disgust at the thin trickle of alkali water emerging from the seep.

Cody chided his horse as he loosened his cinches, then lifted the saddle from Yankee's back and dropped it to the ground.

"Beggars can't be choosers, bud. You should be grateful we're not makin' a dry camp."

When the Ranger slipped the bridle off of Yankee's head, the gelding lowered his muzzle to the waterhole, sucking up the alkaline contents.

Cody took a brush from his saddlebags, rubbed down his paint, then turned him loose to roll and crop at the sparse grass surrounding the spring. Cody had to wait for the seep to refill before he could drop to his belly and duck his head in the tepid liquid. It soothed his sun and windburned face. Cody drank his fill. He pulled out his battered coffeepot and filled it with the bitter water. Taking some fallen mesquite branches, he made a small, nearly smokeless fire. After a supper of bacon and beans, he drank his coffee and doused the flames. Lingering over the brew, he gazed at millions of tiny stars in the black curtain of the night sky. The weary Ranger rolled in his blankets and pillowed his head on his saddle. He said his evening prayers and fell asleep.

Sometime later, a subtle change in his surroundings roused Cody from his slumber. A crescent moon, low in the western sky, placed the hour after midnight. The night creatures were silent. Yankee was outlined against the dim horizon, his ears pricked sharply forward as he snuffed a warning. Quietly, Cody slid his Colt from the holster beside his blankets.

A slim figure moved stealthily from behind a cluster of low rocks. As the intruder approached Yankee, the horse pinned his ears back flat and whickered a sharp warning.

"Hold it right there, or I'll drop you where you stand!"

Cody's voice cut through the silence. The figure jerked to a halt and stood frozen.

"Don't…don't shoot, Mister," a thin voice stammered. "I didn't aim to hurt you."

"Raise your hands, slow and careful," Cody ordered, "and stand still."

"Yes…yes sir, Mister."

The intruder raised his hands, keeping one eye on Yankee who now had his upper lip curled back and his teeth bared. Cody slid from his blankets and came to his feet.

"Step over here. Let me get a look at you. No false moves."

The Ranger's revolver was still aimed at the man's stomach. The intruder carefully stepped toward him. A grunt of surprise escaped Cody's lips. He was looking at a towheaded youth who appeared no more than fourteen. Starlight revealed a stained, flop-brimmed hat perched on the boy's head. His body was encased in a ragged homespun shirt and patched jeans. Run-over boots completed the youth's sorry outfit.

"Mister, I wasn't tryin' to steal your horse," the boy protested. "I was just lookin' for help. I figured I was gonna die out here 'til I heard your horse snort."

"What're you doin' way out here, kid?" Cody demanded.

"A no-good horse thief stole my Brownie and left me for dead," the boy said, then crumpled to the dirt.

*   *   *

"Easy, son, drink this slow," Cody advised, placing his canteen to the boy's lips.

He'd propped the youngster's head against his saddle.

"What...what happened?" the boy stammered.

"You fainted," Cody replied. "Appears you haven't eaten for a while. You've got a real nasty bump on the back of your head. What's your name, son?"

"Tommy. Tommy Mashburn. The no-good jasper who stole my horse gave me that lump."

"Well, you must be powerful hungry."

It was obvious to Havlicek that this emaciated, half-starved boy posed no threat.

"Tell you what. Lemme patch up your scalp, then I'll whip up some grub. You eat and tell me who stole your horse. My name's Cody."

"I'm mighty grateful, Cody," Tommy replied.

After cleaning and dressing the cut on Tommy's head, Cody built a fire. He soon had coffee boiling. The Ranger heated some beans, fried a mess of bacon, and mixed up fresh biscuits.

"The grub's just about ready. You think you're up for my lousy cookin'?"

"Just try me," Tommy answered as he heaped his plate with bacon and beans.

Cody watched the boy eat enough for three grown men. While the Ranger scrubbed out the frying pan and tin plates, the youngster finished his tale.

"I was ridin' east, headin' for San Angelo," Tommy began. "My folks died of the fever a few months back. I tried to hold onto our ranch by myself, but it wasn't much of a place. Then, with the drought…," Tommy shrugged. "There was nothing more I could do. So, I was hopin' to find a cowpuncher's job over thataway. I'd heard a few of the ranches might be hirin'. You got any more of that coffee?"

"Sure do." Cody lifted the pot from the coals and refilled the boy's tin mug. "There's a couple more biscuits left too. I've got to be movin' by sunup. I need to reach Haggerty's Junction before tonight. Finish your story."

"All right," said Tommy. "Yesterday mornin' a big ugly-lookin' feller jumped me. He hit me over the head, knocked me out, and took Brownie."

Tommy's chin trembled.

"She wasn't much of a horse, just an old brown mare, but my pa gave her to me when she was foaled. She was all I had left. The hombre who jumped me must've ridden his horse into the ground, I figure. So he took Brownie and left me afoot."

Cody's eyes narrowed in anger. Fury roiled the Ranger's guts at the thought of any man who would steal a kid's horse and leave him to die.

"I reckon I would've died if I hadn't stumbled on your camp when I did. I was just about finished," the boy said.

"At least he didn't shoot you," said Cody. "You have any idea which way that hombre headed?"

"Westward, toward Fort Davis. Leastwise, I think he headed that way."

"Would you recognize him if you ran across him again?"

"I could pick him out blindfolded. But there's no chance of catchin' up to him."

"There's always a chance," Cody replied. "First though, we've gotta get you back to where there's some folks. Yank'll carry double for a ways, long as I say so. The sun'll be up in a half-hour. Get ready to ride."

Cody packed up his gear and saddled the big paint.

"Tommy, it's a good thing you weren't tryin' to steal my horse," the Ranger said.

The youngster avoided the man's gaze as he flushed deep red.

"Truth to tell, I thought about it. You've been so good to me, I just can't lie to you. I couldn't do to anyone what that jasper who stole Brownie did to me."

"It takes a real man to admit somethin' like that," Cody answered. "Just forget about it. But like I said, it's a good thing you didn't try it. Yank's a one man horse, ain't yeah, bud?"

Cody scratched Yankee's ears. The horse nuzzled his rider's shoulder, nickered, then dropped his head to Cody's hip pocket to beg for his customary peppermint. Cody slipped the treat to his mount and Yankee crunched contentedly.

"Yank, Tommy's gotta ride with us a ways, so you behave yourself," he ordered.

The paint snuffed at the boy's chest, then whickered.

"Okay, Tommy."

Cody stepped into the stirrup and swung onto Yankee's back. Grasping Tommy's wrist, he lifted the boy onto the horse, settling him behind the saddle. As Tommy wrapped his arms around the Ranger's middle, Cody heeled Yankee into a steady trot.

The rising sun gilded the eastern horizon pink and gold. Two miles from his campsite, Cody spied several black specks circling in the cloudless sky. Further on, he pulled Yankee to a halt alongside a dead horse lying off the trail. The Ranger's blue eyes grew cold as he stared at the bloody spur gouges on the bay's flanks. There were also quirt marks on his rump and neck.

"I reckon this horse belonged to the hombre who stole your mare," said Cody.

"You mean he's gonna treat Brownie like that?" the youngster cried out in despair.

"Not if I can help it," Cody muttered. "Mebbe, with any luck, he traded her for another horse at a ranch around here. We won't find him just settin'. Let's go, Yank."

                    *   *   *

Even a horse as tough as Yankee couldn't maintain a hard pace for long while carrying double. It was well after sundown when Cody reined him in atop a rise. The Ranger gazed down at a dimly lit building below.

"That's Haggerty's," he explained to Tommy. "Here the trail to Fort Davis crosses the north-south road to Fort Stockton and Alpine. We'll rest for the night. Mebbe we'll come up with a mount for you."

Cody heeled his gelding down the slope.

"Oats just ahead, Yank," he promised.

They headed toward the ramshackle adobe structure that was the Haggerty's Junction Trading Post. Tommy slumped wearily against the Ranger's back, his head lolling as he struggled to stay awake. Yankee halted at the water trough in front of the building.

"Cody! That's Brownie!" the boy exclaimed, now fully awake.

He stared in disbelief at a small brown mare that stood hipshot at the rail.

"I'm gonna find the man who took her," Tommy declared.

"Just take it easy, son," said Cody.

Tommy slid from Yankee's back, ran up to his horse, and wrapped his arms around her neck. He buried his face in her thick mane. Brownie lifted her head and whickered.

Cody climbed from his saddle and tossed Yankee's reins over the hitchrack. Anger flared in his eyes as he saw the bloody spur gouges on the mare's flanks. Salt and dried sweat encrusted her hide. He lifted his Colt from its holster, spun the cylinder, and checked the loads.

"Tommy, you stay here," he ordered

"Cody, I…"

"I mean it, son," Cody repeated in a tone that would brook no argument. "I'll be right out."

He climbed the worn stairs, crossed the sagging porch, and pushed his way into the building.

Cody worked his way past piles of haphazardly stacked merchandise. The sole occupant, an elderly bespectacled clerk, stared curiously at him. The Ranger headed for the brightly lit barroom off to the right side. Cody halted just inside the entryway, scanning the men grouped at the bar and the card players at three felt-covered tables. Tobacco smoke swirled around the coal-oil ceiling lamps. A few of the patrons gazed indifferently at the newcomer, then turned back to their drinks.

"I'm lookin' for the hombre ridin' that brown mare out front."

Cody's harsh voice cut through the babble of the crowd. One of the gamblers paused in mid-deal, the card he'd just tossed fluttering unnoticed to the table. Silence descended on the room as everyone turned to face the tall figure framed in the doorway.

One of the men at the bar took several paces toward the Ranger. His muddy eyes held a flat challenge.

"I'm the man who owns that mare. What of it?"

Cody ran his gaze over a black-stubble jawed man. Greasy dark hair hung lank under a dirty Stetson. Thick muscles rippled beneath a stained blue shirt.

"Any man who'd ride his own horse to death, then steal a horse from a kid and leave him to die in the desert, deserves stringin' up, that's what."

"I didn't steal that lousy crowbait from no snot-nosed kid," came the surly reply. "I bought that mare from a rancher outside of Sanderson. Don't see what business it is of yours anyhow. You've got no right bustin' in here and accusin' me of horse stealin'."

"I found the kid you stole her from. He's outside with his horse right now. I'm haulin' you to the sheriff, Mister."

At the end of the bar another man challenged Cody. He had a clear shot at the Ranger's ribs. His hand hovered over the big Smith and Wesson hanging at his right hip.

"My pard's been right here with me for the last three days. You callin' him a liar?"

"No. I'm callin' him a horse thief *and* a liar," Cody snapped. "Since you claim he's been here for three days, I reckon that makes you just a plain old liar."

"You're not takin' me anywhere, but you're headed for Boot Hill, cowboy," the first man snarled as he dropped his hand to his gun and jerked his pistol from its holster.

Cody's left hand slashed down and up, triggering his Colt as soon as it was level. He was already diving to his side as his slug ripped into the renegade's stomach. The horse thief doubled up, clawing frantically at his bullet-torn belly. The Ranger twisted and fired again. A bullet from the second outlaw tore through the air and buried itself in the opposite wall. Cody's bullet smashed into the second man's chest, slamming him backwards against the bar. The dying man slowly sagged to a seated position and toppled to the floor.

"Easy, boys," Cody warned, his voice low and deadly.

The smoking Colt in his hand seemed to mark each man in the room for death.

"Let's not make any mistakes here. Anyone who goes for his gun'll end up with a bullet in his middle, just like those two hombres. Bet a hat on it."

"Cody!" Tommy burst through the door.

The boy's eyes widened as he spotted the two gunmen. One was already dead with a bullet through his heart. The other curled up on his side, with hands clamped to his middle, as blood pooled around him.

"I told you to stay outside, kid," Cody growled, without taking his eyes off the stunned spectators.

The acrid scent of powder smoke now mingled with the odors of tobacco, spilled whiskey, and stale sweat.

"Let him stay," said the burly, bearded bartender.

He kept his hands conspicuously away from the shotgun under the bar as he turned to face Tommy.

"Kid! Is what this jasper's sayin' the truth?" he asked the youngster. "Jackson there stole your horse?"

Haggerty jerked a thumb in the dying outlaw's direction.

Tommy swallowed hard, quivering slightly as he stared at the man who'd stolen his horse lying sprawled in the sawdust.

"Yeah," he shakily replied. "He stole Brownie."

"I reckon none of us have any quarrel with you then, Mister," the bartender declared. "Jackson always was no-account. And Riley, his pardner, wasn't much better. Besides, there's not one man in here who'd take the side of a blasted horse thief. I'm Patrick Haggerty."

"I'm Cody…this here's Tommy," the Ranger gruffly answered.

Havlicek punched the empty shells out of the cylinder of his Colt, reloaded the gun, and slid it back into its holster.

"Tate! Mose! A couple of you men get Jackson and Riley outta here," Haggerty ordered and turned back to Cody. "You plannin' on stayin' the night, hombre?"

"Nope. I've gotta get on down the road apiece. I was gonna see about a horse for the kid," Cody explained. "But there's no need of that now. I'll just pick up some supplies and grain for our horses, then we'll be on our way. Besides, I don't care for some of your clientele."

The barroom started coming back to life as the bodies were removed and men resumed their drinking and gambling.

"I can't be choosy about my customers way out here," Haggerty shrugged.

He called to the elderly clerk who was hovering nervously in the doorway of the barroom.

"Henry, take care of this gentleman. See that he gets whatever he needs."

"Appreciate that," Cody grunted to the owner. "C'mon, Tommy, let's get goin'. This ain't a fit place for a young'n."

His hand still brushing the butt of his Colt, Cody backed out of the bar and into the trading post.

*   *   *

After replenishing foodstuff and purchasing a small sack of grain for the horses, the Ranger and boy rode south several miles.

They turned into a small grove of stunted live oaks that surrounded a shallow waterhole.

"We'll camp here for the night."

Cody reined in Yankee and dropped wearily from his saddle.

"We should be far enough out, in case Jackson or Riley had friends who might try and bushwhack us. And we both need shut-eye."

"Sure, Cody."

Completely exhausted, Tommy slid off his worn-out mare. His recovered outfit was an old saddle, an ancient Henry repeating rifle, and a thin bedroll.

"Get that saddle off her and rub her down real good, then we'll see what we can do about those cuts," Cody told him. "Use this on her."

Cody tossed a new brush to the boy and a yellow-painted tin labeled E. E. Dickinson's Witch Hazel.

"After you've brushed the dirt off Brownie, rub her with that."

"What's this stuff?" Tommy asked as he opened the container. He sniffed at the bitter smelling liquid and wrinkled his nose.

"Just what it says, witch hazel. Comes from a shrub that grows all over New England. It'll take some of the soreness out of her muscles and help keep those cuts from gettin' infected"

"Sure, Cody," Tommy agreed, as he loosened his horse's cinches.

He dropped his saddle to the ground, then went to work on Brownie's sweat-encrusted hide. The little mare leaned into the brush.

Yankee nuzzled at Cody's hip pocket for the ever-present peppermint.

"Lemme get your saddle off first, doggone it," he scolded, as Yankee dug harder at his hip.

Cody lifted his saddle from the paint's back and slipped him a peppermint, handing two to Tommy, one for his horse the other for himself. Both mounts crunched on the treats.

Once the horses were brushed, Cody poured out a small portion of grain to each.

"Lemme get to work on Brownie," Cody said as their mounts ate their oats.

"Better be careful," Tommy warned. "Brownie might not take to havin' you foolin' with her after what she's been through."

"You don't have to worry about that. Horses and I just plain understand each other," Cody said. "You stay by her head and talk to her while I patch her up."

The Ranger dug out a tin of salve and a clean bandanna from his saddlebags. Dipping the bandanna in the spring, he used the wet cloth to wash out the spur gouges in Brownie's flanks, then dried the wounds with his spare shirt and coated them with salve.

"Is she gonna be all right?" Tommy questioned.

"She'll be just fine," Cody reassured the boy. "We'll make Alpine by tomorrow night and both of you can rest up there. Let's turn them out, and we'll have our own grub."

Yankee was let loose while Brownie was picketed on a thick patch of grama grass.

"You don't need to hobble your horse?" Tommy asked.

"Nah. He won't wander off," Cody explained. "Yankee's been with me for quite a spell. I took him away from an hombre who was whalin' the hide offa him with a horsewhip. I gave that man a taste of his own medicine. Yank'd been mistreated for quite some time. It took a long while before he'd even trust me. We've been lookin' out for each other ever since."

He looked at Tommy and collected his thoughts.

"We've gotta have a cold camp tonight just in case someone did follow us."

He dug several strips of jerky and a few pieces of hardtack from his saddlebags.

"You really think someone might've?"

"I doubt it. I don't think Jackson or Riley had many friends, and stealin' a man's horse is about as low down as you can get. Still, there's no point in takin' any chances."

"I reckon you're right. And Cody, I didn't thank you for what you've done for me and for Brownie."

"*Por nada.* You gonna be all right after what happened back at Haggerty's?"

Even after years of riding with the Texas Rangers, Havlicek still got sick to his stomach when he had to kill a man. Seeing those two outlaws lying bullet-riddled on the floor of Haggerty's bar was bound to be rough on a boy of Tommy's age.

"I'll be just fine," Tommy replied, his voice shaking. "I know you told me to stay outside, but when I heard those gunshots, I just had to know what happened to you. I'm sure glad you didn't get plugged instead of them."

"I've gotta agree with you there," Cody laughed. "Now, let's get some shut-eye. We'll be ridin' out at sunup."

As they rolled in their blankets, Tommy's curiosity finally got the better of him.

"Cody, what're you doin' out here, anyway?"

"Just driftin', kid," Cody snapped. "It's not healthy to ask a man too many questions like that."

"Sorry, Cody."

Tommy tried to hide the hurt in his voice.

"Forget it," Cody said. "Just get some sleep."

4

Cody and the boy were up and on the trail at first light. He kept
Yankee at a steady pace, putting plenty of miles behind them.

"First thing we've gotta do when we reach Alpine is find you a
place to stay, kid," Cody explained to Tommy as they neared the
town.

Since turning southwest from Haggerty's Junction, they'd been
riding along the base of the rugged Glass Mountains, which pierced
the eastern horizon on their left. Further to the west, the even more
formidable peaks of the Van Horns and Sierra Viejas formed an
almost impenetrable barrier.

"I'd kind of hoped you'd let me string along with you, Cody,"
Tommy replied.

The boy had ridden in moody silence most of the way, becoming
even more morose as they neared their destination.

"I told you, I've gotta keep movin'," Cody answered. "I can't
have you taggin' along and slowin' me down. Don't worry, I won't
just leave you behind to fend for yourself."

Cody smiled at the youngster in an attempt to reassure him.

Tommy returned a thin, nervous smile of his own, but didn't reply.

"We should get to town by late afternoon," Cody continued as
he glanced up at the sun. "C'mon, Yank, get on up there."

He pushed his horse into a fast lope.

*   *   *

About four that afternoon, as he walked a bone-tired Yankee down the main street of Alpine, the image Cody presented was anything but that of a Texas Ranger. His clothes: a faded blue shirt, a red bandanna, jeans, worn leather vest, and scuffed boots were dust-coated and damp with perspiration. He hadn't shaved or had a haircut since leaving Austin. A thick stubble covered his jaw, and his blonde hair brushed his collar. Cody appeared to be a grubline riding cowpoke…or a man one step ahead of the law.

The blue eyes under Cody's Stetson missed little as he continued through the hardscrabble town and headed for the livery stable. With rutted streets, fetlock-deep in dust, the buildings a mixture of peeling adobes and false-fronted wooden structures, Alpine was much like any of a hundred other West Texas towns Havlicek had visited in the course of his Ranger career. A sun-faded sign proclaimed the "Dust Devil Saloon" to be the largest establishment there. Alongside the saloon stood The King's House, a sagging, unpainted hotel in stark contrast to what its name implied, and "Sheriff's Office" marked a sturdily built adobe opposite the hotel.

Cody's gaze lingered with interest on a window which had "Alpine Advisor" stenciled on it. The window held an *"Apprentice Wanted"* sign. A stocky, balding individual in his early forties, wearing an ink-stained printer's apron and green eyeshade, stood in the doorway of the newspaper office. As Cody smiled and touched the brim of his Stetson in a brief greeting, the newspaperman glared at him. The man retreated into his office, slamming the door shut behind him.

Cody grinned briefly at the boy riding alongside him.

"That might be a possibility for you, Tommy," he observed, pointing at the sign.

"I don't hanker to be a newspaperman," Tommy retorted.

"You'd best think about it," Cody advised. "You've gotta find a job doin' somethin', and that'd be a whole lot better'n endin' up tumbleweedin' like me."

The Ranger's voice carried a hardness he didn't feel. Truth to tell, he'd enjoyed having a riding companion and had grown fond of Tommy. But now that he'd reached Alpine, Cody had to lose the youngster, and quickly. Once he'd ridden into town, the Ranger had no way of knowing if he'd be recognized. A bushwhacker's bullet might expose the boy to danger.

"There's the stable just ahead."

Cody pointed out a weathered barn with "Joe's Livery" painted in faded blue letters over the doors. He urged Yankee into a trot.

A thin man of about twenty stepped into view as Cody and Tommy dismounted and led their horses into the shade of the barn.

"I'm Joe Barnes, owner of this place. Stalls for your horses?"

"Yup," Cody replied.

"Whoa! Easy, horse!" Barnes yelped as he reached for Yankee's reins.

Cody's big paint flattened his ears and curled back his upper lip revealing wicked yellow teeth. He lunged at Barnes's stomach.

"You can feed and water mine, but I'll rub him down myself. Yankee doesn't care for strangers. Best you don't touch him. My name's Cody, the boy there's Tommy."

"Don't you worry about that, Mister. I won't go near your horse."

Barnes studied Havlicek as Cody patted his horse's shoulder.

"Yankee? That's a kinda funny name for a Texan's horse," he remarked.

"Not if the horse's owner is also a Yankee," Cody grinned. "My folks and I came down here from New Hampshire when I was just a young'n."

"I knew that wasn't any East Texas drawl you were spoutin'," Barnes answered.

The man laughed as he ran his gaze appreciatively over the Ranger's paint.

"Your cayuse sure is a handsome fella," he observed. "Put him in that third stall on the right. The mare can go in the one next to that. Rate's four bits a day."

Cody dug a coin out of his pocket and handed it to the stableman.

"That's fine. Here's a week in advance. Dunno for sure how long I'll be stickin' around."

Cody jerked a thumb toward Tommy.

"The kid here's gonna be staying in town. I found him in the badlands. His horse was stolen. You know where he might find a job?"

Cody lifted the saddle from Yankee's back, led him into the stall Joe had indicated, and began to rub him down.

"I can take care of myself," Tommy protested as he led Brownie into her stall and removed the mare's bridle.

"Sure you can," Cody replied, "for a day or so. How about it?" he asked the hostler again. "You think the kid can find a job anywhere?"

Joe Barnes thumbed back his battered Stetson and scratched his head thoughtfully before replying.

"I can't use him here. I've barely got enough work to keep myself busy. I'll tell you what, though. He can bunk in the hayloft until he finds somethin'. Wait!" Joe snapped his fingers. "How about the newspaper? Al Kroeger's lookin' for an apprentice."

"I'll find my own job," Tommy retorted. "Besides, that newspaper hombre don't seem very friendly."

"That won't be easy," Joe explained. "It's not roundup time, so none of the ranchers are lookin' for riders. The paper's probably your only chance, less'n you want to sign on as a swamper in one of the saloons. Besides, Kroeger's all right. It's just that he's real big on law and order. He acts that way toward anyone who rides into town lookin' like he might be trouble…not that I'm implyin' anythin' about you, Cody," he hastened to add.

"No offense taken. I've gotten used to folks reactin' like that whenever I ride into a town."

"If I can't hire on at a ranch, then I'll ride out with Cody," Tommy insisted.

"No, you won't, kid," Havlicek snarled. "I've already told you, I've gotta be driftin'. We're partin' ways, here and now."

He turned back to Joe.

"That money covers both horses for a week, right?"

"It'll do."

The hostler glanced at Brownie, then shot Cody a baffled look.

"Mister, I thought you said the kid's horse was stolen?"

"It was," Cody replied. "I got it back."

"Oh." Joe nodded his head knowingly. "Anyway, yeah, that

money'll take care of both animals."

"Good."

Cody dug a half-eagle from his jeans and tossed it to Tommy.

"There, kid, that'll hold you for a couple of days."

Turning his back on the boy, Cody gave Yankee a final swipe of the brush, slipped him a peppermint, then shouldered his saddlebags and Winchester. He walked from the stable trying to ignore the hang-dog expression on Tommy's face.

*   *   *

Cody obtained a room at The King's House and spent the rest of the afternoon napping. As much as he desired a long hot bath, shave, and haircut, he felt maintaining his image as a drifter was more important. He settled for cleaning up with tepid water from the cracked basin and pitcher in the cramped, dingy room.

Just after sundown, at a nearby cafe, Cody ate a steak dinner and headed for the Dust Devil Saloon.

"This had better work," he thought as he pushed through the batwings. "I've gotta get in touch with the sheriff without anyone bein' the wiser."

The Dust Devil was no different than other saloons the Ranger had visited. A mirror-backed bar ran the length of the room, and paintings of women adorned the walls. Card tables were arrayed to one side, along with a faro set-up. Females in low-cut dresses circulated among the patrons. A stairway led to a gallery above from which doors opened onto several private rooms. The tinny notes of a badly tuned piano vied for attention with the rattle of roulette wheels and chuck-a-luck cages. Tobacco smoke drifted up to grimy coal-oil chandeliers. The place reeked of spilled whiskey, stale sweat, and tobacco. Several men turned to stare briefly at the new arrival. Wilting under the steely gaze of Havlicek's blue eyes, customers returned to nursing their drinks.

Cody chose a place at the bar alongside two cowboys. Judging from the volume of their conversation, they had already consumed several drinks. He nodded to them as he waited for the bartender to take his order.

"Howdy, Mister," the man greeted him. "Welcome to the Dust Devil. What's your pleasure?"

"Sarsaparilla," Cody replied.

"Sarsaparilla?" the bartender echoed.

"That's right. Sarsaparilla. You have a problem with that?"

"No!" The saloonkeeper flushed under Cody's steady gaze. "Comin' right up."

He rummaged under the bar and found a bottle.

"One soda pop!" he stated loudly.

The lanky cowboy at Cody's elbow nudged his partner's side.

"Hey Jed! This here jasper's drinkin' soda pop!" He laughed drunkenly. "Nobody I know ain't drunk soda pop since they left their mammy's knee."

"He's drinkin' *what*, Deke?" his partner asked.

"Sassyparilly," the first cowboy replied.

"You got a problem with my choice of drink, pal?" Cody sneered.

"Yup. I sure do," Deke taunted. "You'd best order a whiskey, Mister. Nobody drinks soda pop in this saloon."

"You do, loudmouth. Bet a hat on that."

Cody tossed his drink into Deke's face.

The cowpuncher stumbled back, sputtering in rage. He recovered, came forward, and struck the sarsaparilla man in the face. Cody drove a fist deep into Deke's gut and followed it with another punch to his chin. The man doubled up and sagged to the floor.

A right from Jed slid along the side of the Ranger's jaw. Cody's return blow crushed Jed's lips against his teeth. He smashed a punch to Jed's chin and another to his ribs. Cody set himself and was stopped in his tracks as Jed ducked under the punch and sank his left fist into the Ranger's belly. Cody bent over, gasped for air, and drove his head into Jed's stomach. Wrapping his arms around the cowboy's ribs, he slammed him back into the bar. Jed slumped to the sawdust, moaning with pain.

Deke rose from the floor. He grabbed Cody by the shoulder, whirled him around, and drove a punch into his jaw. Cody staggered and punched Deke in the chest and mouth. Deke's return punch took the Ranger on the side of his head, spinning him around. The Ranger shot a hard blow to Deke's stomach. As the cowboy stumbled backwards, Cody swung at his chin again only to be dropped by the bartender who hit him over his head with a bung starter. Stunned, the Ranger went to his knees.

"My turn, Mister!" Deke growled through bloodied lips.

He sent a vicious kick into Cody's groin. The Ranger crumpled onto his side, writhing in pain. Deke drew a foot back for a second kick into his ribs, but the kick was never delivered. Sheriff Mark Carlisle rushed into the Dust Devil with a sawed-off shotgun.

"Hold it, all of you!" The sheriff ordered, his voice cutting through the shouts and yells of the spectators. "What the devil's goin' on in here, Mike?" Carlisle demanded.

The bartender nodded at Havlicek, who was still doubled up on the floor.

"That hombre there couldn't take bein' hoorawed about his drinkin' soda pop. He started all this."

"That's right, Sheriff. There was no call for it. We was just havin' a little fun with him," Deke agreed.

He lifted Jed from the sawdust and both cowboys leaned against the bar.

"Well, I reckon a night in a cell'll cool him off. C'mon, stranger."

Carlisle yanked Cody's gun from its holster and his Bowie from its sheath and pulled him to his feet. He moved him along by shoving the shotgun's twin barrels into the Ranger's spine.

"Get movin'," the sheriff ordered.

He shoved Cody through the batwings and to the street.

*   *   *

He removed Cody's gunbelt and pushed him into a cell.

"In there, you."

Cody stumbled to the bunk and sat painfully on the edge of the thin mattress.

"You got a name?" Carlisle demanded as the Ranger sagged against the wall.

"It's Smith. Jim Smith."

"Very funny. Well, Mister Smith, or whoever you are, you might as well make yourself comfortable. I've got to finish my rounds. And let me warn you, no one's ever broken out of my jail."

"There's always a first time," Cody retorted. "Reckon I'll just get some shut-eye."

Sheriff Carlisle headed back to the street.

Cody stretched out with a satisfied smile.

"So far, so good," he thought as he pulled off his boots. "Now I might as well get some sleep."

Cody was awakened as the sheriff returned. The lawman barred the office door, pulled down the shades, and turned up the lamp. Carlisle settled in his chair and leaned back. He rolled and lit a cigarette.

"Sheriff," Cody hissed. "I've gotta talk to you."

"I'm headin' for the sack, Smith," Carlisle responded. "I suggest you do the same."

"I need to talk to you *now!*" Cody urgently repeated. "Turn around, Sheriff."

Wary of a trap, Carlisle stood up and lifted his gun from its holster. He stopped, gazing in disbelief at the silver star on a silver circle that the prisoner held in his hand.

"A Ranger?"

"I'm Texas Ranger Cody Havlicek. You can holster the gun, Sheriff."

Carlisle blinked, still not believing his eyes. He slid his gun back into its holster.

"What's this all about?"

"Keep it quiet, Sheriff," Cody warned. "I had to figure out a way to see you without anyone suspicionin' I was a Ranger. That little set-to in the saloon did the trick."

"Kind of hard on you though, wasn't it?" Carlisle grinned.

"Well, things did get somewhat out of hand," Cody admitted, rubbing the lump on the back of his head.

He slid his badge back inside his shirt pocket.

"We'd best talk fast, just in case anyone decides to happen by,"

Cody added.

"You want some coffee? The pot's still warm."

"That'd go down good," Cody replied. "Thanks."

Carlisle poured two cups, passing one to the Ranger.

"Smoke?"

The sheriff held out the makings.

"Thanks, no. Never did get into the habit."

"Suit yourself," Carlisle began rolling another quirley. "Where do you want me to start, Ranger Hav…Havli…?"

"Have-luh-check," Cody said. "Easier to just use my first handle, Cody."

"Okay, Cody. I'm Mark…Mark Carlisle."

He stuck his cigarette between his lips, struck a match, and lit his quirley.

"Tell me what you can about the killin's you've had around these parts," said the Ranger.

Carlisle thumbed back his hat as he pulled up a chair next to Cody's cell. He took a deep drag on his cigarette and blew a smoke ring toward the ceiling.

"They started a few months back. First it was Ross Moore, who owned the harness shop. Everyone, includin' me, figured it was just a robbery gone bad. Then, down to Study Butte, which is right on the Mexican border, Paolo Alvarez was found with a knife in his back. He ran a little jerkline freight outfit, haulin' goods from Mexico to Pecos and back. Finally, about a month ago, Peter Hunt, who owned the biggest ranch in the county, was bushwhacked. That's when I sent my wife to visit her mother in St. Louis. I felt it was too dangerous for Gail to be around here with a killer on the loose. She didn't want to go at first, but her ma's been sick so I was able to finally convince her."

Carlisle took another deep pull on his cigarette before concluding.

"After Hunt was killed, I decided to ask the Rangers for help. One showed up and started nosin' around."

"Chance Lowney."

"That's right. He must've found somethin', 'cause he headed over to Marathon and got himself killed there."

"You have any idea who shot him?"

"Not a clue. The killer ambushed him from an alley."

Cody took the photograph of Lowney's body from inside his shirt and passed it through the bars.

"Have you seen this before?"

"No," Carlisle answered. "Where'd you get it?"

"It was sent to Ranger Headquarters, along with a note warnin' Cap'n Blawcyzk not to send any more Rangers down here. You got any idea who took it?"

"Yeah," Carlisle grunted. "A couple months back a photographer pulled into town. Name's Josiah Anders. Said he was takin' pictures all over Texas. He took that one of me and Gail."

Carlisle jerked his thumb toward the back wall, indicating a framed tintype.

"Anders stayed here for a month, then headed to Marathon. I doubt he's still there, 'specially if whoever shot Lowney knows he took that picture."

"Unless the killer wanted Anders to take that picture," Cody disagreed. "It's worth a chance lookin' Anders up, since I'll be ridin' for Marathon anyway. There was another Ranger sent down here, name of Hap Tompkins."

"Like I wired Captain Blawcyzk, he never turned up. Ben Tate, my deputy in Marathon, never saw him, and he didn't come here. My guess is he must've gotten drygulched by whoever killed Lowney."

Carlisle took a swallow of his coffee.

"Before you ask, Tate didn't see Lowney's killin' either. He was out of town on a wild goose chase, lookin' for some rustled cattle, when that Ranger got it."

"He might've been called out on purpose."

"Could've been," Carlisle agreed. "There's more. Since Lowney was killed, Ted Boscobel was also murdered, found shot in the back behind his feed store here in town."

He sighed in frustration. Their conversation was interrupted by loud voices and boots on the boardwalk. They faded and Carlisle continued.

"There were no real clues left at any of the killin's. And here's another funny thing. The only dead man who's turned up in Marathon was the Ranger. All of the others, 'cept for Paolo Alvarez and Pete Hunt, were killed here in Alpine. And even Hunt was on his way into town when he was ambushed and found the next mornin' with two bullets in his back. Also, Alvarez was on a run from Chihuahua to here when he was killed. There sure seems to be a connection to Alpine somewhere in all this. I've got all the files right here in my desk. You can look 'em over if you'd like."

"I'm not goin' anywhere," Cody chuckled, waving at the bars of his cell. "I can go through 'em tonight. And, sooner or later, I'll figure out why Chance Lowney headed for Marathon and into a bushwhackin'. Bet a hat on it."

"*Sta bueno*," Carlisle agreed. "Cody, I sure hope you have better luck than those other two Rangers."

"So do I," Cody concurred, "since I'm kinda partial to livin'. Mark, I've gotta ride out first thing in the mornin'. A kid name of Tommy rode into town with me. I found him in the badlands where some no-good hombre had stolen his horse and set him afoot. I'd appreciate it if you'd keep an eye on him."

"Sure, I saw him over at the livery. I also heard you got his horse back, and that the hombre who took it won't be stealin' anymore."

"I don't need to remind you it's important no one finds out I'm a Ranger."

"My mouth's shu," Carlisle agreed, then added with a devilish glint in his eyes, "Why don't I plan you a real special send-off?"

*　　*　　*

Slade Hanscom knocked on the back door of a house on the outskirts of Alpine, making sure he was unobserved.

"Who's there?" A voice from inside demanded.

A lamp was lit, casting a soft glow through the kitchen window.

"It's Slade, boss."

"Slade? What in blazes are you doing here this time of night? I warned you never to come here."

The door was flung open and Hanscom sidled in.

"Don't worry. I made sure no one saw me, and this news couldn't wait. Another Ranger rode in today."

"Another Ranger?" Hanscom's employer drew in a sharp breath. "Are you sure?"

"I'm positive. His name's Cody Havlicek. I wasn't sure if it was him at first. But when he picked a fight at the Dust Devil over his drinkin' soda pop, I recognized him for certain. He's kind of an odd duck for a Ranger. He's real soft-spoken and slow-movin' until he gets riled. Havlicek doesn't drink liquor or smoke, and he won't mess with the saloon gals. Any hombre he plugs generally doesn't ever get back up."

"Blast it, this is all we need."

"He's from up north somewhere," Hanscom continued. "He's still got a trace of Yankee accent which is pretty easy to pick up. Plus, he's left handed, so the gun on his left hip kinda sticks out. The real clincher though was when I heard him say 'bet a hat on it' when he started that fight. It's a funny expression Havlicek uses a lot. I asked him about it once. He said it was somethin' his father always said, and that he'd picked it up from his old man."

"This is the first time I've ever heard of a Texas Ranger who's a regular choirboy."

"Havlicek ain't no saint, boss," Hanscom protested. "He enjoys a good game of poker, except he won't play for high stakes, and drops out if the game gets too rich. He's chain lightnin' with his six-gun or fists…crack shot with a rifle, too. Rides a big paint horse that's the devil himself. I saw that horse chomp the guts out of an hombre who had the drop on Havlicek one time."

"Did anyone else ride in with him?"

"Just some kid who's stayin' with Joe down at the livery. He's a stray Havlicek picked up after the kid's horse was stolen. Havlicek got the horse back and let the kid trail him here, accordin' to Joe. I dunno if the kid's aware Havlicek's a Ranger."

"I doubt it," said the boss. "Havlicek wouldn't have told the boy who he was, figuring he'd be bound to brag about riding with a Texas Ranger. We won't have to worry about the kid. And if it turns out I'm wrong, a stray can disappear real easy without anyone asking questions. Where's Havlicek now?"

"In jail," Hanscom replied. "Carlisle ran him in after the fight. I could drill him through the window easy."

"No. Not here in town. Too many questions would be asked. You said Havlicek started the fight?"

"Yeah, he sure did."

"Then I'm almost certain that fight was a set-up so Havlicek could talk to Carlisle without anyone catching on."

"What're we gonna do?"

"This third Ranger ridin' into town tells me for certain they got that photograph I sent to Austin. Obviously, they don't intend to heed my warning. Havlicek will head for Marathon. Send Dixon down there to see Riley tonight. Have him tell Riley to set up an ambush for Havlicek at Reed's Gap."

"That Ranger will never see Marathon," Hanscom promised.

"I'm sure he won't, but just in case he does somehow get through, we'd better have a couple of men waiting for him there."

"I'll have Riley himself take care of that." Hanscom spoke and paused. "How about Carlisle? He's a problem. So's the photographer."

"I'll take care of the sheriff when the time comes," said the boss. "For now, he's exactly where I want him. As far as Anders goes, you're right. However, I understand he's out in the desert taking pictures again. When he returns, he plans on pulling out for the border. We'll wait for him to head for Mexico, then take care of him in the badlands."

"What if Havlicek gets to him first?"

"You're being well paid to make sure that he doesn't. If he should, then Riley will have to kill both of them."

"I'd better find Dixon and get him moving," Hanscom said, "if Riley's men are to make Reed's Gap ahead of that Ranger."

"Do that...and Slade..."

"Yeah, boss?"

"Excellent work spotting Havlicek. You'll be getting a nice bonus."

"Thanks."

"One more thing. If the Ranger does somehow make it to Marathon, we'll need to be careful how we get rid of him. His death must not be connected to us."

"His body will never be found," Hanscom assured his employer.

"Make certain of it. Now get out of here. And go straight home once you see Dixon. No stopping for a drink on the way."

"Sure, boss." Hanscom's voice barely concealed his disappointment.

*   *   *

"Fine, Mr. Smith. Let's see, that was bacon, flour, salt, beans, Arbuckle's, and a box of .45 cartridges. Will there be anything else?"

"I don't think so," Cody Havlicek replied, chuckling inwardly at the fear in Silas Dean's eyes.

Obviously, the Alpine Mercantile's owner was aware the man standing at his counter had spent the previous night in the town jail. Dean, a short, gray-haired cadaverous man in his fifties, wore thick spectacles. He padded around his store like a nervous cat. The Ranger thought him more suited to an eastern university than a general store in a rugged frontier town.

"Wait a minute," Cody ordered as his gaze settled on a jar at the end of the counter. "Better let me have all of those peppermints."

"All of them?" Dean asked.

"Yep, all of them. They can be pretty hard to find out on the trail."

"Certainly," Dean replied. He emptied the jar and counted out the candies. "You must have quite the sweet tooth, Mister Smith."

The storekeeper placed the peppermints in a small sack.

"They're not for me. They're for my horse," Cody explained.

"Your horse? He must be a very special animal."

"He is," Cody chuckled. "He certainly is."

"If there's nothing else, sir, your total comes to $4.26."

"Things are gettin' expensive," Cody complained as he paid the bill.

"Indeed they are," Dean sympathized.

He passed Cody's purchases over the counter.

"If you should ever find yourself in Alpine again, please stop in."

"I will," Cody promised, as he shouldered his package and pushed open the door. *"Muchas Gracias."*

Havlicek stepped out of the mercantile.

"Smith! I thought I told you to get out of town!" Sheriff Carlisle challenged.

"I was just pickin' up a few supplies for the trail, Sheriff."

"Well, just to make sure you don't forget..."

Carlisle drove a fist solidly into Cody's belly, doubling him up. The sheriff's following punch took him on the chin, spinning him off the boardwalk and into the dusty street. Cody rolled onto his back, a trickle of blood at one corner of his mouth.

"Nobody does that to me, Sheriff," Cody growled.

He reached for the Colt on his hip, then halted with the gun half out of leather. Carlisle had already pulled his six-gun, holding it leveled at the Ranger's broad chest.

"Try it, and die right here," Carlisle snarled. "Now get on your horse and ride."

His eyes blazing with fury, Cody slid his Colt back into its holster and dragged himself to his feet. He retrieved his package from where it had fallen into the road, tied it to the saddlehorn, and hauled himself onto Yankee's back. Sitting hunched over in the saddle, he pressed a hand to his middle. Al Kroeger, still wearing the same ink-stained printer's apron, stepped out on the boardwalk with Tommy at his side.

"What's goin' on here?" Kroeger demanded. "Is this a story for my newspaper?"

"This is the saddlebum who started all the trouble in the saloon last night," Carlisle explained. "I'm just makin' sure he knows troublemakers aren't welcome in Alpine."

"That's the kind of law enforcement we need, Sheriff," Kroeger asserted. "Can I get a statement?"

"Soon's I make sure this hombre rides out," Carlisle replied.

"Yeah, make sure he leaves, Sheriff," Tommy bitterly agreed. "We don't need his kind around here."

"So that's the thanks I get after savin' your worthless hide, kid," Cody snarled. "Maybe I should've left you out in the badlands where I found you."

"That's enough out of you," Carlisle snapped, waggling his gun for emphasis. "Get outta here."

"I'm goin'," Cody growled. "But I'll be comin' back for you, Sheriff."

"I wouldn't try it—but I'll be ready to accommodate you anytime you'd like," Carlisle retorted. "Now get!"

"You're holdin' all the aces—for now." Cody grumbled at the lawman.

Yankee backed away from the rail. Cody hunched over and heeled the big gelding into a trot. A stab of remorse passed through him at the pain and disappointment in Tommy's eyes.

"At least the kid got a job," Cody thought. "And that was a pretty good show the sheriff put on. C'mon, Yank, we've got a long day's ride ahead of us."

He touched his spurs lightly to the paint's flanks, putting him into a ground-eating lope.

5

"It'll be easier travelin' once we get through Reed's Gap," Cody said to himself and the horse.

He studied the surrounding countryside as they headed eastward toward Marathon.

"Hardly any greenery on these mountains at all," he noted.

The trail from Alpine veered north at this point. The seven-thousand foot high Ord Mountain continued on and met up with the rugged Glass Mountains. Horse and man climbed steeply.

"I'd like to rest a spell too, Yank," Cody told the lathered paint, "but we need to make town before sundown. Tell you what. Soon's we hit the Gap, we'll take a half-hour *siesta*."

Up higher in the surrounding mountains, it would be cooler, with even a few stands of pines or firs growing in spots. However, at this altitude waves of heat shimmered from the rust and ochre hued boulders lining the trail. Cody squinted against the blinding rays of the desert sun as he and his horse plodded doggedly onward.

"Hold it a minute, Yank."

Cody reined in his mount and pulled off his Stetson, wiping sweat from the inside band.

"That's Reed's Gap just ahead. Time for a drink, boy."

Cody took his canteen from the saddle horn, swung down, and filled his hat, placing it in front of his gelding's muzzle. Yankee drank greedily.

"That's enough for now," Cody chided.

The Ranger climbed back into the saddle, lifted the canteen to his lips…it was ripped out of his hands. A rifle shot echoed from the narrow pass, and a red-hot streak of pain burned its way across Cody's neck.

The Ranger dove from his saddle. He grabbed his Winchester from its scabbard and rolled behind a large boulder. Yankee knew rifle fire and streaked for safety. The big horse screamed in pain, reared high and toppled onto his side, as a bullet struck him. The paint thrashed helplessly for a moment, struggled to rise, then settled to lie unmoving in the dirt.

"Yankee! " Cody shouted.

Tears of rage flowed down the Ranger's cheeks.

"I'll make 'em pay for that if it's the last thing I do," Cody vowed.

He forced himself to stay sheltered until he got his emotions in check, then peered cautiously over the rocks. Instantly, two bullets split the air above his head.

"Two of 'em," he muttered. "Got 'em spotted."

He crawled around the left side of the boulder, threw his rifle to his shoulder, and fired. A bullet ricocheted off the rocks behind him. He ducked, rose up and fired again, and watched the man fall to the rocks below.

"That's one."

Cody rolled back into cover, removed his bandanna, and retied it over the blood-oozing bullet crease in his neck.

"Now to make the other snake crawl out of his hole."

Cody jacked another shell into the chamber of his rifle. He jumped to his feet, zigzagged across the trail, and slid on his stomach into a shallow ditch. As he rolled behind a cluster of ocotillo, a rifle slug took off one of the plant's wands, just over his head. Cody snapped a shot in return and grunted in frustration as his bullet missed.

"Gotta end this right now," he muttered as another bullet plowed into the dirt just behind him. "That hombre's gettin' the range. He's gonna nail me right quick. 'Sides, I'm just about out of bullets."

Cody's spare ammunition was in the saddlebags on his downed horse.

"Here goes."

Acting as if he were running away, Cody leaped to his feet, and ran forward. Then he dove to his belly, rolled, and squeezed off a shot. The second drygulcher screamed and his rifle fell from his grip. The gunman slid down the slope and sprawled lifeless up against a clump of prickly pear. A thin haze of dust marked his path.

His rifle still at the ready, Cody walked numbly to where Yankee lay on the trail. A pool of blood darkened the dust around the gelding's head. The rugged Texas Ranger dropped to his knees alongside his horse and stroked Yankee's neck.

"Yank, I'm sorry, bud." Cody said.

He buried his face in the paint's thick mane. When he did, Yankee's body quivered violently and the horse lifted his head.

"YANK! You're not dead!" Cody exclaimed as his horse struggled to his feet.

Cody wrapped his arms around the paint's neck. Yankee stood and nuzzled his companion.

"You'd better let me take a look at you."

Cody examined the bullet slash between Yankee's ears. To his great relief, what he had thought was a fatal wound was merely a deep crease.

"You're gonna be all right, boy! I'll patch you right up."

Cody dug the containers of witch hazel and salve from his saddlebags. He flushed the wound, then coated it thickly with salve. As he finished, Yankee nuzzled at his owner's hip pocket, begging for a treat.

"Sure, you can have a peppermint." Cody laughed as he gave him one. "You can have as many as you want. For awhile there, I thought I'd never be givin' you candy again."

He patted Yankee's muzzle.

"You take it easy while I check on those two hombres," he ordered.

The horse followed along as Cody walked up to the last ambusher and dragged him from the prickly pear. He rolled him onto his back. A crimson stain spread around the bullet hole in his stomach. Cody stalked over to the other gunman whose dead eyes stared unblinkingly into the blazing sun.

"Neither one of these hombres is gonna talk," Cody told his horse as he finished going through the men's pockets. "No clues on either of 'em as to who they are."

He headed back to where his canteen lay in the dust and kicked the bullet-punctured vessel in frustration.

"We'd better find their horses and hope for a full canteen. Can you give a whinny, Yank?"

The big paint lifted his head and whistled piercingly. An answer echoed down the pass.

"Good work, pard," Cody praised. "Let's go get 'em."

It only took a few minutes to find the renegades' horses, which were tied in a clump of mesquite just off the trail.

Cody grunted in satisfaction as he sloshed the contents of two almost full canteens.

"We've got water, anyway. How about you, bud?" he questioned his horse. "I'd best ride one of these broncs for a bit until you're feelin' better."

Cody untied the reins of a chunky bay mare. Yankee snorted angrily and shoved the other animal aside.

"All right, all right, I get the hint," Cody conceded. "I reckon you're feelin' just fine."

He stripped the gear from the dead men's mounts, gave them a short drink, and turned them loose.

"Guess the act the sheriff and me put on back in Alpine didn't work," Cody remarked.

He climbed into the saddle and urged his horse to a slow walk.

"It seems like we've been spotted, Yank. 'Course," Cody laughed as he glanced at the paint's chestnut and white splotched hide, "you've always been spotted."

Yankee's only response was a snort. Behind them, several buzzards were already circling in their slow descent.

*   *   *

"That'll be Marathon just ahead, Yank," Cody murmured.

The sun hung directly at their backs. The lengthening shadows pointed straight at the buildings emerging from the heat-shimmering valley ahead.

"We'll put on the feedbag in a little while," Cody said. "Tell you what. Since we'll most likely have a welcomin' committee watchin' for us, it'll be better to hit town after dark. We'll wait here and get some rest."

He reined the gelding near a sheltering clump of mesquite and yucca.

Cody tied Yankee loosely to a stunted bush. He looked about for critters and laid down his bedroll. Stretching on the ground, he pulled his Stetson over his eyes. He thanked St. Francis of Assisi for protecting his horse and himself, and fell asleep.

Cody awoke just after sundown, allowed Yankee a quick drink, then gulped down some warm water himself. After rolling the bedroll and tightening the cinches, he swung into the saddle and headed down the trail to Marathon.

Near the edge of town, Yankee, sensing oats and a comfortable stall, picked up his pace.

"Easy there, pard," Cody cautioned. "I'm lots hungrier'n you are. At least you had grass to chew on. Let's find that stable."

A few minutes later, the Ranger was dismounting in front of Barrett's Livery.

"Help you, Mister?" an elderly hostler asked the stranger.

"You sure can," Cody smiled. "A stall and feed for my horse. Make sure he gets plenty of hay and water. I'll rub him down myself. Yank doesn't take to very many folks."

"I can see that," the hostler replied as Yankee pinned back his ears. "The rate's two bits a night. Put him in that first stall."

Havlicek dug in his pocket, pulled out a coin, and tossed it to the stableman.

As Cody led Yankee down the aisle, the man stared at the bullet crease on the horse's head.

"What happened to him?"

"He got that from a low-hangin' branch of a live oak," the Ranger lied, knowing the salve would disguise the wound. "He's a tough ol' bronc; he'll be just fine."

"What's your handle, stranger?" the hostler asked. "Mine's Bob."

"I'm Cody."

He lifted the saddle from Yankee's back and began brushing the paint.

"You plannin' on bein' in town long?"

"Depends," Cody shrugged

"The Drover's Hotel is the best in town. 'Course, it's the only hotel in town," Bob offered. "As far as grub, you can't go wrong with Tricia's Place. Trish serves a mean steak, and she's pretty easy on the eyes to boot."

"What does a feller do for fun?"

"For drinks most of the cowpokes head for the Trailsman. Don't try the Silver Nugget, less'n you want to tangle with a mean bunch of miners."

"Mind if I ask you a question?"

"Shoot."

"I noticed a storefront sign that read "Photographer"across the way. You folks got a picture taker in this town?"

"We sure do," Bob replied. "I understand he's gonna be driftin' on in a few days. Right now, he's somewhere out in the desert."

"I've always wanted to get my picture taken. Mebbe I'll look him up when he gets back."

Cody gave Yankee one final swipe with the brush, then slapped him on the shoulder. He turned to the stableman.

"Thanks for your advice," Cody told Bob as he closed and latched the stall door.

"Always glad to help a stranger," the hostler replied, "and don't fret about your horse."

"I always do," Cody grinned.

He shouldered his saddlebags and Winchester and headed for the hotel. As soon as he could, he ducked into an alley. He watched Bob leave the stable and go into the Trailsman Saloon.

"Well, Ranger," Cody murmured to himself. "Your arrival in Marathon won't go unnoticed. You can bet a hat on that."

*   *   *

The room Cody obtained at the Drover's Hotel was spartan and clean. There he left his saddlebags and Winchester and headed for the cafe. Tricia Ann Dowd, the redheaded owner, served him supper. After a final slab of apple pie, Cody went over to the Trailsman Saloon.

It was Saturday night and the barroom was crowded with cowboys and ranchers from off the range. Cody managed to find a place at the bar where he could keep an eye on the room. A brassy blonde wearing a low-cut sapphire dress, touched his elbow.

"Howdy, stranger," she drawled.

She ran her gaze boldly up and down the Ranger's lean form.

"You're new in town. Care to buy a lady a drink? My name's Lila and I can make sure you won't be lonely while you're here."

"No! Right now I'd just like to cut the trail dust from my throat."

"I could make it worth your while," Lila purred.

"I'm not interested, lady. I've had a long, hard ride. All I want is a couple of drinks and a good night's shut-eye."

"Suit yourself, Mister! You're probably not as good as you look anyway."

"Probably not," Cody chuckled.

The woman flounced away. She found and wrapped her arms around the waist of a lanky cowpuncher.

"It seems you made the lady mad," one of the bartenders laughed.

"She seems to be takin' it well," Cody replied.

"She does at that," the man agreed. "Welcome to the Trailsman. I'm Steve Pardee, the owner. What's your pleasure, cowboy?"

"The name's Cody. And I'll have a sarsaparilla."

"One ice-cold sarsaparilla comin' right up," Steve grinned.

He ducked into a back room and returned a moment later with several bottles and a glass.

"I figure'd you'd want more'n one, Cody," he explained as he placed the bottles on the bar. "Just don't get too drunk on this powerful brew."

The Trailsman's owner grinned as he filled Cody's glass.

"Never do," Cody answered.

He spun a coin on the bar. His request for sarsaparilla was met with only a slightly raised eyebrow from the cowboy next to him. Cody glanced around the smoke-filled room, seeing no sign of Bob from the stable or anyone else he recognized. He engaged several cowboys in friendly conversation. None seemed too interested in Havlicek's business, nor provided much information to his discreetly worded questions. Most of the patrons concentrated on their drinks, card games, or danced with the female entertainers. Cody's gaze settled on a door to the rear of the saloon marked *Private.*

"Sure wish I could get a glimpse in there," he mused. "Mebbe I'll stick around awhile longer."

Cody stood at the bar for about an hour as he studied the occupants of the saloon. His interest was piqued when one of the card players at a nearby table pushed back his chair.

"I'm done for the night, fellers," the player said in disgust. "My luck's gone cold. Mebbe I'll try again next week."

The unlucky player strode out of the Trailsman. Cody wandered to the vacant seat and nodded to the men at the table.

"Interested in a game of poker, cowboy?" asked one of the men.

"You might talk me into it," Cody grinned. "Cody Havlicek's the name."

"Miles Thibodeaux," the gambler smiled.

Thibodeaux was a well-proportioned Creole in his late thirties. He wore the usual garb of his trade, a freshly pressed black broadcloth suit, a boiled shirt, and a black string tie. A bulge in his jacket indicated he wore a shoulder holster and pistol under his left armpit.

"Pleased to make your acquaintance," Thibodeaux declared. "This here pretty lady is my good-luck charm, Yvonne Waters."

"Ma'am." Cody touched the brim of his Stetson in a polite greeting.

Yvonne was a tall, willowy woman, with a flawless complexion. Her raven hair flowed freely over her shoulders. She smiled at the tall Ranger, her red lips parted just slightly to expose dazzling white teeth.

"These gentlemen are Trace Hopkins, Dave Hastings, and Moe Levin," Thibodeaux finished.

Hopkins and Hastings were ranchers, both in their thirties. Levin was the owner of the general store.

"Five card stud's the game," Thibodeaux told Cody. "Nothing's wild, and the stakes are four bits a bet, unless you're searchin' for somethin' larger."

"That's fine with me," Cody agreed. "Start dealin'."

While he played poker for the next few hours, Cody kept watch on the door to the private room. The only person who entered or left the chamber was one of the bartenders.

Cody was a few dollars ahead when he pushed back his chair, yawned, and stretched.

"I'm done in, fellas," he announced. "I've been on the trail a long while. It's high time I got some shut-eye."

"Are you sure, Cody?" Moe Levin queried. "Your luck's better than mine."

Even with the low stakes, Levin had dropped quite a bit of cash.

"I'm certain," Cody replied. "I'm plumb worn out. Maybe another time."

"That'd be fine," Thibodeaux smiled. "But it'll have to be in the next few days. I'm gettin' ready to pack up and head for Alpine. There's too much trouble in this town since that Ranger was killed."

Thibodeaux gazed shrewdly at Havlicek.

"I guess that's one thing us gamblers and cowpunchers have in common. We just can't hang our hats in one place for any too long. Good night, Cody."

"I reckon you're right," Cody laughed. "'Night, fellas."

Cody went to his room and turned in for the night.

*   *   *

As Cody played cards, he was the object of intense discussion by the occupants of the back room.

"That's Havlicek, the Ranger, no doubt," Ned Riley flatly stated. "Bob got it right."

"That means he got past Cleve and Mace. He must've downed 'em both," Riley said as he muttered a cursed.

"You don't think there's any chance Bob might've been mistaken?" Monte Harris asked.

"No," Riley replied. "His description of that blasted lawman matches Slade's."

"That's him, all right, and he's settin' there big as life, playin' cards and suckin' down soda pop," Luke Rafferty said.

He stepped back from the door's peephole. With a curse, Rafferty hitched up the gunbelt sagging at his hip.

"I'm gonna take care of that Ranger once and for all, right here and now!"

Riley's voice cut through the thick air as Rafferty placed his hand on the doorknob.

"Hold it, Luke! You know we can't have any more killin' here in town…especially another Texas Ranger. You just let me worry about takin' care of Havlicek."

"Ned, I've been waitin' more than three years for this chance," Rafferty protested. "Havlicek arrested my kid brother…and had him hung, just 'cause he killed a coupla' Mexican goat herders."

Luke Rafferty pounded his fist on the wall in anger.

"Worse, Havlicek's testimony sent me to prison for cattle rustlin'. I vowed while I was in Huntsville that I was gonna kill that lousy Ranger."

"You can kill him when we're ready," Riley answered, "but when and where I say. *Comprende?"*

"No! I want to see the look on Havlicek's face when I plug him," Rafferty snarled, turning to leave.

Riley pulled his six-gun from its holster and leveled it at Rafferty's back.

"You won't get outta this room if you try it, Luke. Just open that door if you don't believe me."

Monte Harris and Jorge Randado also had their guns out and pointed at Rafferty's spine.

"You won't pull that trigger," Rafferty challenged. "The shots'd bring that Ranger runnin'."

"Sure they would," Riley replied. "But it wouldn't matter to you, Luke. You'd be dead. Then we'd kill Havlicek. He'd join you in

Hell."

Rafferty stared at Riley's pistol for a moment and turned from the door with a resigned shrug.

"You're holdin' all the aces, Ned," he growled. "Guess I've got no choice."

"Don't worry," said Riley. "Havlicek's all yours when the time comes. We just need to make sure it's done right. Now, let's finish our card game. We'll head for the ranch later and figure out how to take care of the Ranger."

Rafferty picked up a bottle and took a long swallow.

"I'm not gonna wait very long," he warned, and then took another drink.

*   *   *

"We won't get much done today," Cody mumbled to his horse. "It's Sunday, so I'm gonna head for church. We'll take a look around after that."

He saddled the big paint and mounted. He guided Yankee to the old Spanish mission at the edge of town.

Arriving at the church, Cody dismounted and looped his gelding's reins over a hitchrail in front of the ancient adobe structure. He hung his gunbelt from the saddlehorn, secure in the knowledge it was safe. Yankee would attack anyone who tried to take it.

Cody stepped into the interior of the old mission, its sanctuary dimly illuminated by scores of flickering votive candles. He paused in front of a statue of Our Lady of Guadalupe. He lit a candle and prayed for the safety of his family and fellow Rangers. Afterwards, he sat in a rear pew as the Mass began.

For nearly an hour, Cody immersed himself in the timeless Latin words and the ritual of the ageless service. He took great comfort in this brief respite from his violent work as a Ranger. The Mass reminded him that most folks were basically decent. He needed that anchor in his life.

All too soon the Mass was over, and Cody stepped out of the dark sanctuary into the blinding sunlight.

"Ranger!"

Cody stopped and blinked in a vain attempt to clear his vision. Luke Rafferty stood thirty feet before him in the bright light.

"Rafferty?"

"That's right, Havlicek. I've been waitin' a real long time for this. Too long. You're gonna die today, Ranger."

"This isn't the time or the place, Rafferty. Not in front of the church. Besides, I'm not armed. My gunbelt is on the horn of my saddle."

Cody heard the parishioners behind him moving out of the way.

"Git it, or I'll plug you anyway."

"I'm not gonna do that, not here."

An elderly padre came up to Cody's side.

"You are a *Rangero Tejano?*" the priest queried.

"Si, Padre. Por favor, stay back."

"I cannot, my son," the priest replied.

The brown robed priest lifted his voice.

"Senor," he called to Rafferty. "This is the Lord's house—and the Lord's day. I will not permit any violence here."

"Then stand aside, old man, or I'll drill you too," Rafferty threatened.

"*Padre,* it's no use. Please let me handle this," said Cody.

"There must be no killing on church ground," the priest answered and stepped in front of the Ranger.

"Rafferty," Cody called. "I'll face you anywhere and anytime you say, except for here. You don't want to kill a priest."

"I reckon he's got no part in this. Meet me a hundred yards up the street. That good enough for you?"

"It'll do," Cody replied. "*Padre,* make sure no one follows me. There's no sense in anyone else gettin' hurt."

"Is there another way to stop this man?" the priest asked.

"No, *Padre.* Luke Rafferty's a wanted killer. He won't let himself be arrested. I've got no choice."

Cody reached his horse, lifted his gunbelt from the saddlehorn, and buckled it around his waist. He checked the action of his Peacemaker, then slid it loosely back into its holster.

"You wait here until I call you," he ordered the paint.

Cody closed the distance between himself and the killer. The gunman stood in the middle of the street, his dark eyes glittering with hate.

"You've got no old man's robes to hide behind now," Rafferty sneered.

"That old man's got more sand in his craw than you'll ever have," Cody taunted. "It takes a heap of guts to stand up to a low-down backshootin' coward like you."

He kept walking toward the gunman.

Rafferty's right hand hung above the pistol on his hip.

"I'm gonna gut-shoot you, Havlicek, and watch you die real slow."

"You're under arrest, Rafferty," Cody called as the distance between them narrowed to thirty feet.

"Go to blazes, Ranger!" Rafferty snarled and reached for his gun.

Cody drew. Both men's pistols blazed as one and the gunfire echoed down the street. Rafferty clamped his left hand to his belly, staring in disbelief. Crimson spread across his shirt, three inches above his belt buckle.

"You...you ain't beat me yet, Ranger," he stammered, struggling to lift his pistol.

Cody fired again. Rafferty's gun flew from his hand as the impact of the slug spun him around and pitched him face first into the dirt.

Cody reloaded his Colt and dropped it back into its holster. He walked over to Rafferty. The padre came and knelt beside the dead man and looked up at the Ranger.

"No matter what else he might have been, he was one of God's children," the priest explained. "I will pray for him."

"Of course, *Padre,*" Cody replied.

He dug his badge from his shirt pocket and pinned it to his vest. A stocky man in his early twenties, wearing a deputy's badge, pushed his way through the gathering crowd.

"What's goin' on here?" the deputy demanded.

"I'm Texas Ranger Cody Havlicek and that's Luke Rafferty. He tried to kill me. I shot faster."

"I can see that," the deputy replied. "Ranger? I saw you ride in last night. I'm Ben Tate. This Rafferty hombre wanted?"

"He was."

Tate turned to the gathering crowd.

"Okay folks, the excitement's over. Go on about your business. Wait! A couple of you men carry the body down to the undertaker's."

The crowd drifted off and Monte Harris slipped unnoticed into the livery stable. He retrieved his horse and rode through the back alleys until he reached the edge of town. For several miles, he ran his horse until he came to a halt in front of a large ranch house. A group of men in the yard stared at him.

"Ned inside, Zeke?" Harris asked.

"He's still sleepin' off last night," Zeke warned. "Best not wake him. You know how ugly Ned gets after he's been drinkin'."

"This can't wait," Harris responded.

"Ned, wake up, quick!"

A moment later, Ned Riley stumbled bleary-eyed out of the bedroom.

"You'd better have a real good reason for wakin' me up so early, Monte," he rumbled.

"I've got one, but you ain't gonna like it," Harris retorted. "Luke couldn't wait. He must've snuck back into town, and he braced that Ranger first thing this mornin'."

"Blast that Rafferty," Riley snapped. "I should've known he'd pull somethin' like that. Where's he at now?"

"At Sterling's Hardware, bein' measured for a pine box. Havlicek put two slugs in him, dead center."

"Hang it all!" Riley cursed. "The boss ain't gonna like this."

*   *   *

After Luke Rafferty's body had been taken to Dalton Sterling, undertaker and proprietor of Sterling's Hardware, Cody and Ben Tate walked to the town marshal's office to talk.

"Coffee?" Ben asked.

He cut a chunk from a plug of tobacco and shoved it into his mouth.

"I sure could use some."

"Comin' right up."

Ben lifted a chipped enamel pot from the stove, filled a tin mug, and passed it to the Ranger. The deputy shifted the tobacco in his cheek and spat a long stream of brown juice into the cuspidor alongside his desk.

"I thought another Ranger'd be comin' into town after the last one got himself killed," Ben explained. "Sure didn't figure you for one when you rode in, though. I would've checked up on you last evenin', but I had to break up a brawl at the Silver Nugget. That took up most of my night."

"I wouldn't have admitted I was a Ranger last night anyway," Cody replied. "I was kinda hopin' to stay incognito."

The Ranger glanced at the badge still pinned to his vest.

"I guess that doesn't matter now since the shootout with Rafferty. Someone must've spotted me in Alpine. A couple of hombres tried to drygulch me at Reed's Gap."

"I take it they won't be any more trouble."

"Nope." Cody took a long swallow of his coffee. "Ben, tell me about the killin' of Ranger Lowney."

"There's not all that much I can tell you," Ben shrugged. "He was only in town for a couple of days when someone cut him down from the alley next to the bank. He took two .45 slugs in the chest. There were no witnesses, at least none that'll admit seein' anything. And Lowney died without sayin' a word to anyone. I was checkin' out a report of rustlin' at the Cross R when it happened. Rode back into town real late that night."

"How about this?" Cody slid the photograph of Lowney's body from inside his shirt and passed it across the desk. "You ever seen it before?"

Ben sighed deeply.

"No, I haven't seen that picture. I did know it existed. Josiah Anders took it right after Lowney got plugged. Where'd you get it?"

"It was sent to Ranger Headquarters along with a warnin' not to send any more Rangers to Brewster County. Someone must've paid Anders for that photo. You have any idea who it might be?"

"I wish I did. Anders drifted out of town the next day. He does that, heads out into the badlands to take pictures. He rode back about a week later, sent some mail, bought supplies, then headed right out again."

"And you never saw him talk to anyone?"

"He just howdy'd a few folks is all."

"Ben, this is important. Did Anders mail anythin' before he left town the day after Lowney was ambushed?"

"Come to think of it, he did," Ben replied. "In fact, he mailed just one envelope, about the size of that picture. Dunno where he sent it, though."

"Even the Rangers can't get that information from the post office," Cody muttered. "You have any idea when Anders might return?"

"You can never know for sure, but he's about due."

"I can't chance waitin' on him. He's my one lead to whoever killed Chance Lowney. If I can track down that hombre, I might be able to figure out who's behind all these other killin's. For all we know, Anders has been drygulched already. I've got a hunch he knows too much. I'm gonna see if I can pick up any sign of him. You got any notion where he might have headed?"

"He usually travels into the Glass Mountains," Ben answered, letting loose another stream of tobacco. "He's got a burro to carry his stuff and rents a horse from the livery. He always takes the same gray mare."

"What's he look like?"

"A little on the short side, kind of pudgy. In his late thirties or early forties, I'd say. Wears an old flop-brimmed hat. You'll have a devil of a time findin' him in those badlands. Nothin' but lizards, rattlers, and dry brush out there, Ranger."

"If he's there, I'll find him. Bet a hat on it," Cody answered.

"You want me to ride along with you?" Ben asked. "I know the territory better'n you. Lived here all my life."

"No. I want you here in case Anders returns. If he does, make sure he doesn't leave town until I get back. Jail him if you have to."

"All right. Anythin' else?"

"One more thing. You had many newcomers to town lately?"

"You mean besides you?" Ben laughed. "The only ones I can think of are the new men at the Cross R Ranch. Lem Tucker, who owned the place, broke his neck when he fell off his horse. Some syndicate from back east bought it from his widow. She moved to Kansas City."

"You met the new owners?"

"No. They've never come out here. A couple of months back, an hombre named Ned Riley rode into town claimin' he was the Cross R's new foreman. He had the papers to prove it. He brought in a tough crew, but you need a tough bunch to run that place. There's rustlers and occasional Comanches that still cross the line from Mexico."

"You know any of the others?"

"Yeah. Luke Rafferty, the jasper you plugged today, just hired on with them. I'd plumb forgotten about that. Riley'll be good and sore when he finds out what happened."

"I'll handle Riley," Cody said. "Any others?"

"Let's see," Ben said, rubbing his jaw thoughtfully. "There's Monte…Harris is his last name, I think. A half-breed named Jorge Randado. Couple of others, Cleve Reed and Macy Purdy. There's a couple more whose names I'm not sure of, and most likely one or two I haven't run across. In fact, most of those boys were in town last night."

"I didn't see Rafferty," Cody protested, "and I would've known him right off."

"They were in the Trailsman's private room," Ben explained. "That eastern syndicate must pay real well, 'cause the Cross R outfit generally uses it whenever they're in town."

"I sure wish I'd known that," Cody said. "How do I find the Cross R?"

"It's about seven miles west of here. Take the Alpine road six miles, and you'll see a fork to the left. There's a Cross R sign on a dead cottonwood stump at the fork. The place is about a mile down that left-hand trail. It sits in the foothills of the Glass Mountains."

"Which is where you think Anders was headed. He may have ridden straight into the rattler's den."

"You think Riley's tied up with these killin's? Why?" Ben asked.

"Only a hunch. And you just gave me a reason."

"I did?" Ben questioned, clearly puzzled.

"Sure. You were out at the Cross R on a wild goose chase when Chance Lowney was gunned down. That was mighty convenient for them."

Cody pulled the badge from his vest and dropped it into his shirt pocket.

"Whoever killed Lowney already knows there's another Ranger in town," exclaimed Cody.

He grinned at Ben as he pushed himself up from his chair.

"But there's no point in givin' him a nice, shiny target to shoot at. *Adios,* Ben. With any luck, I'll see you in a couple of days."

"Vaya con Dios, Ranger, and good luck."

6

They were about five miles out of Marathon when Cody's normally sure-footed gelding jammed his off front hoof between two rocks, springing the shoe and pulling it half off. Cody picked up Yankee's leg and examined it carefully, noting to his great relief there appeared to be no torn ligaments nor strained tendons. However, the shoe was bent beyond repair, so badly twisted Yankee refused to put any weight on his foot.

"Dadblast you, Yank," Cody scolded his horse. "Why'd you have to pick now to decide to jam a hoof?"

Using his thick-bladed Bowie knife, the Ranger pried the shoe off completely and tossed it aside in disgust.

"I guess we've got a long, hot walk back to town ahead of us," Cody observed, glancing up at the blazing sun. "I can't chance lamin' you by ridin' without that shoe. We might as well get started."

*　　*　　*

Two hot, dusty hours later, Cody hobbled down the main street of Marathon with Yankee limping alongside him. The Ranger's feet were raw and blistered, his clothes drenched with sweat, shirt clinging to his back.

"Let's see if we can hunt up the blacksmith, Yank," Cody said to his horse as he led him into the livery and called for Bob.

The hostler shuffled out from the small room that doubled as his office and living quarters.

"What happened, Ranger? Horse throw a shoe?"

"Not exactly," Cody replied. "He caught his foot in some rocks. Any chance of gettin' that shoe replaced right away?"

"Not until mornin', I'm afraid," Bob replied. "Beau Manning's our blacksmith, but he's got a hard and fast rule about workin' on Sundays. He just won't do it. Besides, you look tuckered out."

"I reckon you're right," Cody conceded. "It'll probably do my horse some good to rest that leg. I'll rub him down, put on some liniment, and you give him a good feed and waterin'. I'll be back first thing in the mornin' and take him to Manning."

"You know where to put him. I'll feed and water him, then I'm gonna head over to the Trailsman and wet my whistle."

Cody led the paint into his stall, pulled the gear off him, and proceeded to rub him down. Bob filled the manger and left a bucket of fresh water for the horse.

"You might be goin' to wet your whistle, Bob," chuckled Cody to himself. "But you're also headin to tell them that the Ranger's back in town."

Cody watched Yankee work on his ration of grain.

"You've got the right idea, pard," he said as he scratched the gelding's ears. "I reckon my feet'll last a while longer, leastwise until I can get some supper. I'll see you in a bit."

Yankee merely lifted his head for a moment, then went back to munching his oats.

Cody crossed the street and climbed the steps to Tricia's Place, limping heavily as he entered the cafe. He settled wearily on a stool at the counter.

"Ranger Havlicek, what in the world happened to you?" the owner asked.

She placed a full pot of coffee and a mug in front of him.

"I really look that bad, huh?" Cody grimaced.

"Like you've been ridden hard and put up wet," Tricia answered as she filled the mug.

Her sparkling green eyes and motherly manner made him feel right at home.

"My horse pulled a shoe. I had to walk back into town, about five miles or so."

"Perhaps some coffee will help. What can I get you?"

"I don't want you to put yourself out, Miss Tricia," Cody answered. "I know you're just about ready to close up."

"Pshaw! It's no trouble. I've never turned away a hungry man yet. How about a nice thick steak?"

"Sounds mighty fine, make that a double order."

"Coming right up," she said, heading into the kitchen.

A few moments later, the tantalizing aromas of frying meat and potatoes filled the cafe.

*   *   *

After finishing his meal, Cody headed for the stable to retrieve his saddlebags and rifle. He turned into the alley leading to the barn; the sharp whinny of an infuriated horse came to his ears.

"Yank!" Cody exclaimed and ran into the stable.

Yankee reared angrily. His forehooves lashed out at a bearded cowboy who held a rope around the horse's neck. The man's hat was missing, and the right sleeve of his shirt was torn completely off. Blood streamed down his arm. Yankee's tormentor pulled a gun from his holster and aimed it at the paint's head.

"I'll teach you, you spotted demon!" the man cursed.

The would-be horse thief never saw Cody. The Ranger dove and wrapped his arms around the cowboy, forcing him back against a post. Cody sank a fist into the man's stomach. Recoiling, the Ranger smashed him backwards with a right to the chin. The cowboy spun a full circle, fell through the door of Yankee's stall, and landed on his back at the horse's feet.

Yankee lowered his head and bared his teeth. The cowboy screamed as the gelding tore a chunk of flesh from his stomach. Yankee lunged at the man again, biting off most of his right ear.

"That's enough, Yank! Stop!"

Cody yelled as his horse bared its teeth for another bite.

"He's had enough, I said!"

He dragged the man away from the infuriated horse. The gelding snorted angrily. Cody pulled the thief to his feet, jerked out his Colt, and rammed its barrel into the man's belly.

"Don't. Don't shoot, Mister," the man pleaded. "I…I didn't know what I was doin'. I was half-drunk and took a likin' to that fancy paint when I saw him."

He cringed as he saw death in Havlicek's eyes.

"Please, don't shoot, Mister!"

"I'm sorely tempted to," Cody snarled. "It's what a low-down thief who'd shoot a man's horse deserves. I'm a Texas Ranger and I should arrest you."

"A Ranger!" the man cried. "I didn't know that paint was no Ranger's horse. You gonna have me hung?"

"I should," Cody growled. "But I reckon you've had enough. I'll give you five minutes to get on your horse and get outta town."

"Can't I see the doc first? I'm bleedin' to death!"

Blood was oozing freely down the man's arm and stomach and running copiously from his torn ear.

"All right," Cody conceded. "I'll give you half an hour."

"I'll leave as soon as I'm patched up."

"Good. Now head for the doc's, then start ridin'. I run across you again and I'll let Yank finish what he started."

"You won't ever see me again, Ranger," the cowboy promised. "And thanks."

The man staggered out of the barn and into the darkness.

"Yank, let's get you cleaned up," Cody said. "You sure took care of him. I doubt he'll try stealin' any more horses."

Yankee nuzzled the Ranger's hip pocket, begging for a peppermint. Cody chuckled despite himself as he scolded the paint.

"Oh no, not tonight, horse. I didn't bring the peppermints with me."

Yankee snorted and buried his muzzle in Cody's belly, shoving the Ranger backwards. Cody grunted.

"I reckon you'll never change," he conceded. "At least I don't have to worry about you ever bein' stolen."

Cody pulled the rope from his horse's neck, found a rag, and dipped it into a bucket of water. He washed the blood from Yankee's head.

"There, that's better. Now I've gotta try and clean this place up."

He washed the blood from the walls, then scattered fresh straw on the floor. The Ranger picked up his saddlebags and Winchester.

"G'night, Yank. I'll see you in the mornin'."

Cody's anger was fading. Havlicek's horse was his one weak spot. Anyone found abusing the paint was bound to face the Ranger's fury.

Cody staggered wearily up the stairs to his room. He stumbled through the door, locked it, and lit the lamp. He pulled off his boots and socks to look at his raw, blistered feet. Taking a tin of salve from his saddlebags, he coated them with the ointment. Too exhausted to remove his gunbelt, he sank back onto the thin mattress and fell asleep.

*   *   *

Cody awakened the next morning to the sun's rays streaming through his window. More worn-out than he realized, the Ranger slept far later than he intended.

He stepped gingerly across the floor to the washstand and splashed water over his face and neck. Wincing with the effort, he pulled on his socks and boots. The pain of his blistered feet had subsided considerably. He limped only slightly as he left the hotel and went to retrieve his horse.

"Mornin', bud, how you doin'?" Cody called to Yankee as he stepped into the stable.

Yankee whickered a greeting and went back to nuzzling a gray mare in the next stall.

The rear door of the barn slid open and Bob entered, carrying a shovel and pitchfork.

"Howdy, Ranger. You're a mite later'n I expected."

"Slept a lot longer than I planned," Cody admitted as he gazed thoughtfully at the gray mare.

"Bob, Ben Tate told me that photographer rents a gray mare

from you whenever he goes on a picture-takin' foray. This the one?"

"That's her," Bob confirmed. "That's his burro, too, in the stall next to her. Anders must've gotten in late last night."

"You don't know what time he got in?"

"Nope. Most of my regular customers just put their horses up themselves if they get in late. If you want to look up Anders, he'll most likely be in his shop. He sleeps in a room off the back."

"Appreciate that. I'd better get this guy his new shoe first," Cody replied.

He took Yankee's halter and lead from a peg, then slipped it over his gelding's head.

"C'mon pard and thanks. If you hadn't pulled that shoe, we'd've missed Anders."

Manning's Smithy was only a few doors from the livery stable. The shop door was open to catch any vagrant breeze. Beau Manning looked up from his anvil and stepped outside as Cody looped Yankee's lead over the hitchrail.

"Can I help you, Mister?" the smith asked.

Manning, stripped to the waist, bulged with muscles under the heavy leather apron he wore.

"My horse pulled a shoe yesterday. I need it replaced as soon as possible."

"You must be that Ranger fella." Manning replied, extending a huge right hand. "I'm pleased to meet you."

Cody grinned as the smith took his hand in a powerful grip.

"Cody Havlicek's the name. Just call me Cody."

"Sure thing," Manning replied. "I can get to your horse soon's I finish up that there team."

He indicated a pair of matched draft horses.

"You gonna leave him here, or wait for him?"

"I've got a couple of things I'd like to get done," Cody responded. "Depends on how you and he'll get along. Yankee isn't easy to handle."

"We'll get along just fine, won't we, Yank, ol' fella?"

Manning ran a gentle hand over Yankee's shoulder. Cody's paint pinned his ears, then relaxed.

"That's a good boy," Manning soothed Havlicek's horse, then smiled at the Ranger.

"Haven't met a bronc yet who didn't like me."

"Well, if Yank takes to you, then you're a rare man indeed," Cody praised. "Long as you two are hittin' it off, I'll leave him in your care. Be back in a couple of hours."

"He'll be ready for you," Manning promised. "Don't fret about him."

"Guess I won't have to," Cody replied.

He watched in disbelief as Yankee submitted to the huge blacksmith's gentle touch.

*   *   *

Cody was anxious to meet the photographer. He would start by asking him to take his picture. Before he could do that, he needed to take a bath and put on clean clothes.

"Besides," he thought, "Anders got in late and he won't be going anywhere. If he does Ben, the deputy, will stop him."

He brushed the dirt from his Stetson and boots, then dug clean clothing from his saddlebag. Leaving the hotel, he crossed the street and entered Fred's Tonsorial and Bathing Parlor. After a shave and haircut, Cody settled into a zinc tub full of hot, soapy water. He spent a moment relaxing while reading a month old edition of the *Alpine Advisor*, a copy lying next to the tub.

"Sheriff Carlisle was right. Al Kroeger's sure big on spoutin' off about law and order," Cody muttered.

He read a rabid front page editorial about how the Texas Rangers were unable to solve the murders of several prominent citizens, killings which had taken place in the newly organized Brewster County.

"Let's see what else is written."

The rest of the four page weekly was devoted to local gossip and the prices of beef and minerals. Cody's attention was drawn to the legal listings, which contained notices of several recent real estate transactions.

"Looks like Silas Dean's been doin' right well for himself," he observed.

The Alpine Mercantile's owner had purchased both Ross Moore's harness shop and Ted Boscobel's feed store. Apparently both previous owners had died. Cody tossed the paper aside as he settled more deeply into the tub, soaking out the aches and grime of the long trail. Then hurriedly, he ran a rough washcloth over his lean body, scrubbing hard. Refreshed, he climbed out of the tub, toweled himself off, and dressed in his clean outfit.

A few minutes later, Cody pushed through the doors of Josiah Anders' photography studio. Anders emerged from a back room to politely greet his visitor.

"Good morning, sir? May I help you?"

Havlicek's nose wrinkled at the odor of chemicals permeating the room.

"Howdy. Are you the photographer?"

"Indeed I am. Josiah Anders, at your service."

Anders' voice held the trace of a Midwestern accent. He looked over the freshly groomed Ranger.

"You desire a photograph?"

"I'd like one for my wife and children," Cody answered.

The lawman flipped the sign in Anders' window from *Open* to *Closed*, turned the door latch, and lowered the shades. He grabbed a piece of paper and scribbled *Busy With A Customer* and placed it next to the closed sign.

"Why are you doing that?" Anders asked nervously. "Other customers may come by. There's no need to be embarrassed, I assure you."

"Town folks are watching," Cody replied. "Let them think I'll be your only customer this morning."

He turned to face the photographer. The star on silver circle now glittered on his chest.

"I'm Texas Ranger Cody Havlicek."

Anders sighed deeply, his gaze fixed on the badge.

"I knew this moment would come. I'll cooperate with you as best I can, Ranger."

"Fine. You can answer my questions while you take my picture."

Anders was taken slightly aback at Havlicek's request.

"You really want a portrait taken?" he asked, raising an eyebrow in bewilderment.

"As I said, for my wife and children," Cody assured him.

"Then we'll start right away. Take that seat, please, while I prepare my equipment. It only takes a few moments."

Anders indicated a straight-backed chair in front of a white screen. As Cody sat down, Anders took a photographic plate from a shelf and slid it into his camera. He picked up a flash pan and powder and placed them alongside.

"Now, how would you like to pose?" he queried. "I suppose standing with your six-gun pointed straight at the lens?"

"No gun, no standing. I'd just as soon do this sittin' down. I had a long walk yesterday, and my feet are still sore."

"Fine. Then let's get to work."

Cody pulled out the photograph of Chance Lowney's body and passed it to Anders.

"Before we get started, tell me about this. You did take that picture, didn't you?"

Anders grew deathly pale as he stared wide-eyed at the image.

"Where on earth did you get this?"

"You didn't answer my question," Cody snapped.

"All right," Anders whispered. "Yes, I took that photograph."

"Now we're gettin' somewhere. I want you to tell me everything you can about the night Ranger Lowney was killed."

"There's not much to tell," Anders replied. "I was working late that night, developing some plates, when I heard shots. That in itself is not all that unusual here in Marathon. I paid no attention to them…that is, until someone knocked on my door. He shouted that a Texas Ranger had just been gunned down, and that I should come with my camera."

"Do you recollect who called you out that night?"

"Of course. It was Monte Harris."

"Monte Harris from the Cross R?"

"Yes, that's the man."

"Keep talkin'."

"When I arrived at the scene of the shooting, quite a crowd had gathered. No one had moved the Ranger's body."

"Do you recall anyone in particular bein' there that night?"

"Harris, of course. Jorge Randado also, along with several other riders from the Cross R. The shooting took place down the street from the saloon, and there were cowboys from several ranches looking on."

"But Monte Harris informed you about the shootin' and told you to bring your camera?" Cody asked. "It must take some time to set up your gear to take a picture at night. Look how long it's taking you to get your equipment ready right now. Yet no one disturbed Lowney's body that night until after you were done?"

"It does take time," Anders agreed. "But as you say, no one interfered."

"Is that 'cause they wanted to stay out of the way, or because Harris and Randado made sure they did?"

"What are you implying, Ranger?"

"Nothing…yet," Cody answered. "Tell me what you did with the picture."

"The next morning, I sent it to Albert Kroeger up in Alpine. He runs the newspaper there, and he's very concerned about the crime in Brewster County. I thought perhaps he would use it along with an account I wrote of the Ranger's murder."

"You sent it to Kroeger?" Cody repeated.

"Absolutely. He mailed me a draft by return post in payment."

"And you didn't send a copy to anyone else?"

"Of course not. Why do you ask, Ranger?"

"Because this photograph was sent to Ranger Headquarters, along with a warning not to send any more Rangers to Brewster County. It was never printed in the Alpine newspaper."

"It must have been," Anders protested.

"Then why hasn't Sheriff Carlisle ever seen it?" Cody demanded. "And, why don't you have a copy of the issue it was in?"

"I don't know," Anders answered.

"Try this on for size. That picture was mailed to Austin from right here in Marathon, not Alpine."

"It couldn't have been," Anders disagreed. "I assure you, I mailed it to Mr. Kroeger personally. There must be some mistake, Ranger."

"For your sake, you'd best hope you didn't make one, Mister Anders. If I find out you know who killed Ranger Lowney, I'll make sure you're charged with obstructing justice and as an accessory to murder."

"Ranger, all I did was take that photograph and send it to Mr. Kroeger. I have no idea what happened to it after that."

"I'll take you at your word for now," Cody answered, "and I assume you still have the plate."

"I do," Anders replied. "It's in my files."

"Then I suppose someone might have gotten their hands on it while you were out in the desert and made another copy. That could explain the picture Headquarters received."

"It could, but I doubt there's anyone in Marathon who would have knowledge of the process. It's rather complicated."

"How about Al Kroeger? Is it possible he might have ridden in from Alpine and made a copy?"

Anders looked despairingly around his studio.

"He may know the process, I suppose. But how would he know where to find the plate? He could hardly ride into town unnoticed."

"True. Still, it's a possibility. Or else Kroeger, or someone workin' for him, might've simply ridden back with your photograph and mailed it to Austin from here. You'd best hope I come up with somethin'. Otherwise, the finger points right back at you, Anders. I strongly advise you not to leave town until my investigation is finished."

"What do I do in the meantime?"

"For now, I suggest you take my picture. In fact, once you've done that, I'd also like one of me with my horse."

"I'd be pleased to oblige," Anders agreed.

*　　*　　*

Promising to return that afternoon, Cody headed from Anders' shop back to Beau Manning's. Yankee whickered noisily as soon as he spotted his rider, while the burly blacksmith greeted the Ranger with a smile.

"Your horse is all set, Cody."

"Thanks, Beau. Did Yank manage to behave himself?"

"He was a true gentleman. I gave him that new shoe and reset the others for you."

Cody laughed.

"That's the first time I've ever heard Yankee referred to as a gentleman," he said. "He's been called a lot of things, but gentleman sure ain't one of 'em."

Yankee placed his nose in the middle of the Ranger's back and gave him a shove.

"Hey, easy you!" Cody shouted.

"I guess he showed you." Manning chuckled.

"He usually does. So how much do I owe you?"

"Six bits and we're even."

"Fine."

As Cody dug in his pocket for the money, Yankee nuzzled insistently at his hip pocket.

"All right, all right, you can have your doggone candy," Cody said.

He produced a peppermint and gave it to the horse.

"Sorry Beau," Cody apologized. "He can be a real pest at times."

"He's also your best friend, I'll wager. He's sure some horse," Manning replied.

"That he is," Cody agreed. He handed a silver dollar to the smith. "The change is yours."

"Thanks. There anything else I can do for you?"

"Mebbe there is," Havlicek replied. "Do you recall anything about that night the other Ranger was ambushed?"

Manning shook his head.

"I wish I could help you, Cody, but once I close up shop I go home to my wife and kids. Usually don't even stop for a beer at the saloon. I never heard about the Ranger's killin' until the next mornin'."

"How about the Cross R men? Can you tell me anythin' about them?"

"Just that they're a good bunch to stay away from. Sure wish I could be of more help."

"You've been plenty of help already, Beau. Take care of yourself."

Cody grinned as he swung into the saddle.

"Let's go, Yank. Time to get your picture taken."

*   *   *

Havlicek always thought better on horseback. After getting Yankee's photograph taken, he rode aimlessly through the rest of the afternoon. He pondered on what he'd learned so far and puzzled over what to do next.

"None of this makes any sense, Yank," he told the gelding as they rested alongside a small stream.

Cody stretched out on his back beside the creek's bank with his boots off and his Stetson tilted over his face. His horse nibbled contentedly on tall grass.

"If Anders is givin' me a straight story, that newspaperman, Al Kroeger, has to be mixed up in Chance Lowney's murder," Cody reflected out loud to himself. "This ties Kroeger into the other killin's and Hap Tompkins' disappearance. That just doesn't add up. And it's lookin' more and more as if the Cross R is somehow connected to this whole mess.

"Anders appeared to steer me away from those boys. Why would he say he knew a Ranger was gonna show up to question him if he only sent that picture to the Alpine paper like he claims? Did he know anything else about Lowney's killin'? He'd have no way of knowin' the picture was sent to Cap'n Blawcyzk, 'less he knows more than he's lettin' on. It's almost as if he was expectin' me all along. And how about Ben Tate? He seems like an honest enough lawman, but mebbe he rode out of town because he knew Lowney was gonna be bushwhacked. There's way too many loose ends here, hoss," Cody complained in frustration.

"Tell you what. The first thing in the mornin', we're headin' back to Alpine. I want to have a long talk with Al Kroeger. Then I want to check the county land records to find out who owns the Cross R.

Sure wish I had more to hang on those jaspers."

Cody sat up and pulled on his boots. He replaced the bit in Yankee's mouth, tightened the cinches, and swung into the saddle.

"We might as well head on back and get some rest. We've got a long ride ahead of us in the mornin'," Cody told his horse.

* * *

After arriving back in Marathon, Cody put up his horse and returned to Josiah Anders' studio.

"Ranger, I have those photographs ready," Anders greeted him. "You make a good subject, I must say. Take a look."

"This is fine work," Cody agreed. "You've managed to make me look almost presentable, and Yank looks downright handsome."

He laughed.

"Now, I'll need your address to send these off."

"I'll send them to Ranger Headquarters myself, just to be safe," Cody answered.

"Okay, Ranger," said Anders.

He wrapped the photographs in brown paper and tied them with string.

"I tried to recall anything that might be of help to you. I'm afraid I had no luck."

"I appreciate that," Cody answered. "I'll be headed out of town in the mornin'. I still don't want you leavin' here until you hear from me or Deputy Tate."

"I'd planned on moving down to Study Butte in a week or so," Anders said. "I suppose that can be postponed."

"Thanks," Cody replied. "Here's the money for the pictures. I'll stop by in the mornin' just in case you come up with anything."

"I'll see you then."

Cody went back to the Drover's Hotel, where he obtained stationery and a pencil. He composed a letter to Sarah and the children and enclosed the photographs. After mailing his package, he spent the rest of the afternoon in a chair in front of the hotel. He observed everyone who passed by. Josiah Anders never left his studio, and no one from the Cross R put in an appearance. Cody had supper with Ben Tate. He liked the young lawman, but did not divulge his conversation with Anders. After two quick sarsaparillas at the Trailsman, Cody checked on his horse and went to bed.

Sometime after midnight Havlicek was awakened from a sound sleep by someone pounding on his door.

"Fire! Fire!"an insistant voice shouted.

Instinctively, Cody rolled out of bed, grabbed his revolver from its holster, and hit the floor. The door was kicked in and a knife flashed through the air, plunging into the mattress where Cody had lain. Cody triggered his Colt, and a man doubled over and fell to the hallway floor.

Havlicek came to his feet. A second man pushed into the room, wielding a knife. Cody stepped back, barely avoiding the razor-sharp blade. He grunted in pain as the knife sliced along his lower ribs and belly. He shoved his pistol against his attacker's stomach and pulled the trigger. The heavy slug blasted the man backwards into the door frame.

Cody grabbed his jeans and pulled them on, buckling his gunbelt around his hips. He leaped over the dying man in the doorway and raced barefoot and shirtless down the smoke-filled stairway onto the boardwalk. The cries of "Fire!" were growing louder, and flames illuminated the street.

"It's the photographer's place!" someone shouted as the Ranger broke into a dead run.

Flames were rolling from the windows of Anders' shop as Cody reached it. Thick black smoke billowed into the air. Men had already formed a bucket brigade and were dashing pails of water against the burning building. This, in a futile attempt to stop the conflagration. Cody grabbed one of the men by the shoulder and spun him around.

"Is Anders still in there?" Cody screamed.

"Dunno, but if he is, he's a goner," the man replied. "Hey, you can't go in there!"

Cody ran onto the porch, slammed open the door, and ducked into the burning building. Choking on the thick, chemical-laden smoke, eyes burning, Cody searched desperately through the front room.

He turned as he heard a wracking cough. Kicking aside a burning timber, he found Josiah Anders sprawled on the floor.

Weakened by the thick smoke and intense heat, and losing blood from the knife slash across his middle, Cody tried to lift Anders. Unconsciousness threatened to overcome him at any moment. Using the last of his strength, the Ranger grabbed Anders under his arms and dragged him across the floor and outside. The building's roof fell in with a roar and collapsed in a shower of flame and sparks. Completely spent, Cody toppled to the road, rolling onto his back to gulp in huge draughts of cool air.

"Someone get the doc," Cody managed to croak.

Several spectators pulled him and the photographer further from the blazing building.

Cody lay flat on his back until he could draw sufficient fresh air into his lungs. After a few moments, he struggled to his hands and knees and crawled over to where Josiah Anders lay.

"Ranger?" Anders had regained consciousness.

His eyes glazed with pain and blood trickled from a deep gash in his scalp.

"I'm right here, Anders," Cody replied. "Take it easy. The doctor's on his way."

"No…No time," Anders gasped. "Gotta…talk."

The photographer coughed convulsively, red foam flecking his lips.

"Files. Steel box. Under the floor. Randado…Harris."

"Try to relax and breathe," Cody urged as Anders struggled to speak.

"Have to. Listen, Ranger, I…"

The photographer broke into another wracking cough.

"I…"

Havlicek leaned closer to Anders' lips futilely attempting to catch his final words.

"What are you tryin' to tell me?" he urged.

Anders lifted his head, trying in vain to form words that refused to come. As his body quivered one final time, the photographer gasped out a long sigh and went slack.

"Sure wish you could've finished what you were tryin' to say," Cody muttered in frustration.

He forced himself upright, swaying dizzily with the effort. Ben Tate elbowed his way to Havlicek's side.

"Cody! You'd better sit down and let Doc Tarbell here have a look at you."

He indicated the gray-haired gentleman beside him, who carried a black satchel.

"I'm fine, Ben," Cody insisted. "But it's too late for Anders."

He nodded at the photographer's body.

"You mean after the foolhardy stunt you pulled runnin' into that building, he was already dead?" the deputy demanded.

"Not quite," Cody replied. "And that fire didn't kill him. Somebody caved in Anders' skull, then deliberately set the fire to try and cover up the killin'."

The Ranger doubled over as he coughed deeply, spitting out a stream of black phlegm.

"You'd better come to my office and let me check you, Ranger," Doctor Tarbell insisted. "Smoke poisoning can be tricky, and you appear to be losing considerable blood from that wound in your abdomen."

"The doc's right, Cody," Ben agreed. "Besides, you're likely to catch your death of cold runnin' around like that."

"Doc, I've got no time for that right now. There's two dead hombres in the hotel I've got to see about," Cody snapped.

"What d'ya mean, there's two dead men in the hotel?" Ben demanded.

"Have a couple of men take Anders' body to the undertaker's, and I'll explain on the way," Cody answered.

*   *   *

The desk clerk at the Drover's abandoned his post to help fight the fire. The two lawmen walked unchallenged through the hotel's empty lobby and up the stairs. Just outside Havlicek's room the body of one of the would-be killers lay slumped against the corridor wall.

"You recognize this hombre, Ben?" Cody asked.

"I sure do. That's Logan Burke, one of the Cross R hands. What's goin' on here, Cody?"

"Soon as I figure it out, I'll tell you."

Cody stepped into his room where the second ambusher lay face-down on the floor. As the Ranger rolled him onto his back, the man groaned and his eyes flickered open.

"That's Zeke Muldoon, another Cross R rider!" Ben exclaimed.

Muldoon stared uncomprehendingly at Havlicek.

"Ranger!" he choked out. "You're supposed to be dead!"

"I'm not that easy to kill."

Muldoon clamped his hands over the bullet hole low in his belly and grimaced in pain. Blood trickled through his fingers as the outlaw glared accusingly at Cody.

"You…you plugged me…in…my…guts, Ranger. That was…lowdown. My…belly…feels like…it's…on fire."

"You didn't give me much choice," Cody retorted.

"Where's Logan?" Muldoon gasped.

"He's dead," Cody answered, "and *you* don't have much time. You have anythin' you want to say before you cash in?"

"I'm not gonna…die from some no-good lawman's…slug."

"Listen, Muldoon, I'm givin' it to you straight."

The man moaned as a fresh wave of agony shot through his middle. His eyes were bright with pain.

"You'll never…get out of town…alive, Ranger. Randado and Harris. They dead…too?"

"Randado and Harris?" Cody echoed.

"Then you didn't get…them," Muldoon exclaimed. "They'll get you, just like they got…they got…"

"Got who?" Cody demanded.

Muldoon's voice trailed off.

"Tell me, Muldoon. Got who?"

"You can go to the devil, Ranger."

Muldoon cursed, doubled up in agony, and curled on his side. He stopped breathing and his eyes rolled back.

"Looks like he got there first," Ben said dryly.

"That's two men who died on me tonight before they talked," Havlicek commented.

"So what's our next step?" Ben questioned.

Cody gazed out the window as the gray light of the false dawn spread across the horizon. He stepped over Muldoon's body and sat on the edge of his bed. He glanced at the knife still stuck in the mattress.

"First, I'd better get dressed proper," Cody said.

He took his bandanna and pressed it to the oozing wound. He put on his shirt and pulled on socks and boots.

"Have someone get these two bodies outta here," the Ranger commented. "As soon as it's light enough, I want to dig through what's left of Anders' shop."

"You really think there'll be anything left to find?"

"Can't tell until we have a look-see. Once I'm done there, it's high time I took a ride to the Cross R."

"What about the doc's?" Ben insisted. "You're lookin' kinda pale."

"You're not gonna give up until I see him, are you, Ben?"

"Not a chance."

"Then we might as well get it over with. Let's go."

*　　*　　*

"This is going to sting, Ranger," warned Doctor Tarbell. "I still wish you'd take some laudanum."

The physician lifted a bottle of carbolic solution from a shelf and opened it.

"And I explained to you, I can't chance havin' my senses dulled, Doc," Cody insisted.

He was lying stripped on an examining table in the back room of Tarbell's small clinic. The peppery physician prepared to work on him.

Tarbell fixed Havlicek with a steady gaze.

"You can't say I didn't warn you. That wound is going to take quite a number of stitches. As it is, you're extremely fortunate it isn't any deeper. If it was, you'd be lying in a coffin, rather than on this table."

The knife slash Zeke Muldoon had inflicted on the Ranger ran from just over his left hip, across his belly, and ended under his navel.

"Just get at it, Doc," Cody muttered.

Tarbell went to work with the calm efficiency of a man who'd spent years treating bullet or knife wounds. Cody grimaced with pain as the doctor washed out the slash, doused it with carbolic solution, and stitched the ragged edges together. Once he bandaged the wound, he ordered the Ranger to sit up.

"I'm nearly finished, but I want to listen to your lungs. You breathed in a lot of smoke," Tarbell explained.

Cody swung his legs over the edge of the table.

"I take in more smoke than that every time I go into a saloon," he protested.

"Nonetheless, humor me," Tarbell replied.

He placed his stethoscope to Havlicek's chest.

"Quiet, so I can listen to your heartbeat and check your lungs," Tarbell ordered.

"Well, Doc?" Cody asked.

The physician lifted the instrument from his chest.

"I really should insist you remain here for a day or two, Ranger. You do have some congestion in your lungs. But, I realize I'd just be wasting my breath…or are you going to surprise me?"

"Not a chance," Cody retorted. "Besides, what could be better for a man's lungs than fresh air?"

"I can't argue that point," the doctor conceded. "You can get dressed. Keep that wound on your abdomen clean, and be careful not to break the stitches. You'll need to have them removed in about a week."

Cody quickly dressed and paid the physician. He opted to spend the rest of the night on a bunk in one of the jail cells.

*   *   *

"Well? What happened in town?" Ned Riley demanded the minute Monte Harris and Jorge Randado stepped into the Cross R ranch house.

"Anders is dead, and his shop's nothin' but a heap of ashes," Harris reported. "Nobody's gonna be able to find what's left of him, or anythin' in that shop either."

"What about that lousy Ranger? Where's Burke and Muldoon?"

"We dunno, boss," Randado answered. "They never met up with us like they were supposed to."

Randado took a bottle of whiskey from the cupboard, uncorked it, and took a drink.

"You didn't look for them?"

Riley's voice shook with anger.

"Take it easy, Ned," Harris urged as Randado passed him the bottle. "We couldn't go back into town with everybody stirred up tryin' to fight that fire."

"That's exactly why you should've gone lookin' for 'em, you dumb idiots," Riley snarled. "With everyone at the fire, nobody would've paid any attention to you. I can't believe you're both that stupid."

"Watch who you're callin' dumb idiots, Ned," Randado warned. "We couldn't do much for Muldoon and Burke anyhow, I figure."

He grabbed the bottle from Harris and took another pull.

"I'm pretty sure I saw Havlicek runnin' out of the hotel," he continued. "So if those boys didn't meet us, and they didn't make it back here by now, they're either dead or in jail."

"Which means that Havlicek'll be ridin' out here as fast as his horse can carry him," Riley growled.

Randado smiled malevolently as he lowered the whiskey bottle, slid his knife from its sheath, and ran his thumb along the razor-sharp blade.

"I'll handle that Ranger."

"Not so fast," Riley ordered. "I want to talk to him first. Then I'll take care of him myself. You two head on over to the bunkhouse and get some shut-eye."

7

The sun had barely poked over the eastern horizon before Cody and Ben were digging through the smoldering ruins of Josiah Anders' photography studio. Several early rising bystanders watched them curiously as they lifted charred timbers and shoved aside heat warped equipment.

"Have you got any idea what the heck we're lookin' for, Cody?" Ben held a prybar borrowed from Beau Manning.

"Anythin' that looks interestin'," the Ranger replied as he sifted through a mound of ashes.

"You never know what might be a lead. Before he died, Anders said somethin' about a steel box hidden under the floor. I wonder where?"

"There probably won't be much left, even if we do find it," Ben pointed out.

"Mebbe, mebbe not," Cody grunted as he pushed aside the heat-twisted frame of a metal chair. "Let's see."

The Ranger ran his gaze over the still-smoking rubble.

"Back there, Ben."

"Where?"

"Anders slept in a room off the back. I'll bet he kept the box under the floor in that room. We might get lucky, since the fire didn't burn quite as heavily there."

"I'll go you one further. I'll bet it was under the bed," Ben replied.

"You're right," Cody exclaimed. "That's gotta be it."

Both men worked their way over the piles of debris to where the sagging frame of a brass bed stood amongst the ruins. They pushed the bed aside.

"You got any idea where to start?" Ben questioned.

"One board's as likely as another. Just start pryin' them up."

"Sure thing."

Ben slipped the end of the prybar under a board, the scorched wood squealed in protest as he lifted.

"No luck under this one," Cody stated.

He found nothing but sand.

Ben lifted another plank with the same results.

"No luck under this one either, Cody."

"Nope. We might have to rip up the whole floor," Cody muttered.

Ben's muscles bulged under his shirt as he pried up an entire section of charred floorboards.

"See anythin'?" he asked.

"I sure do." Cody reached far into the cavity under the floor and removed a scorched metal box. "This has to be it. I'd bet a hat on it."

"C'mon, open it," Ben urged as he hunkered alongside the Ranger.

Cody nodded at the bystanders.

"Not out here. There's too many pryin' eyes and ears. Tell you what, Ben. Let's head back to your office, and I'll fix some breakfast. We'll open this box and check the contents where no one can see."

"If there's anythin' left," added Ben.

"We won't know until we open it, and I'm so hungry I could eat a bear," Cody responded. "A few more minutes waitin' to open this box won't make any difference."

"I reckon you're right," Ben agreed, "and I'm starved myself."

A short while later, after downing heaping plates full of bacon and eggs, they sat at Ben's desk. Before them were steaming mugs of black coffee.

"C'mon Cody, open that box. What the heck are you waitin' for?" the young deputy urged.

"Curiosity killed the cat and more'n one overly nosy lawman,"

Cody laughed.

He took his knife and slid the heavy blade under the lid and lifted. One quick twist, and it popped open.

"Sure don't look like much," Ben observed.

Cody pulled out a few sheets of charred, crumbling paper.

"Can't say, until I read 'em over," Cody replied as he unfolded the first sheet. "Nothin' much on this one. It's only a receipt for photographic chemicals."

He unfolded the next sheet of paper.

"Well, Cody?"

Ben rounded the desk and stood behind the Ranger, trying to read over his shoulder.

"Nothin' here either. Let's try the next one."

"That looks like another receipt," Ben observed, as Cody lifted the paper from the box and carefully opened it.

"It is, and this is what we're lookin' for!" Cody exclaimed.

"What've you got there?"

"It's a draft receipt from one, Albert Kroeger, who runs the newspaper in Alpine. It's in payment for the picture of Chance Lowney's body. Kroeger paid Anders a thousand dollars for that photograph."

"A thousand dollars? For a picture? That doesn't make sense," Ben stated.

"It does if Anders knew more than he was lettin' on. He told me the only thing he did was sell that picture to Kroeger. Claimed he didn't know anythin' else about what happened to Lowney. Let's see what this tells us."

Cody removed the last sheet from the file and unfolded it, struggling to read Anders' almost illegible scrawl on the heat-singed paper.

"What's it say, Cody?"

"Gimme a minute."

The Ranger scanned the last few lines. He leaned back in his chair and took a long swallow of coffee before he replied.

"It's hard to make sense of it, between the bad handwritin' and the fire damage. It looks like Anders had a good idea who killed

Chance Lowney—and he knew Kroeger was tied in with his murder. It seems Anders is the one who sent the photo of Lowney's body to Austin, at Kroeger's orders."

Cody squinted as he strained to decipher the rest of the letter.

"This says somethin' about Kroeger havin' a pardner. It appears Anders was tryin' to blackmail Kroeger and his pard. That must be the reason he held onto these papers."

"So that's why Anders was killed," Ben flatly stated.

"That's only part of it, I'd guess," Cody replied. "Our law and order newspaperman might've been stringin' Anders along until he had no more need for him. When I showed up and questioned Anders…"

"That photographer had to be eliminated," Ben concluded, "and so did you, Cody. Let's ride out to the Cross R and arrest those snakes."

Ben's eyes blazed. He shoved another plug of tobacco into his mouth and worked it between his cheek and gums.

"None of this explains the other killin's, and we still don't know what happened to Hap Tompkins," Cody reminded the deputy. "I'm not even sure we've got enough evidence to arrest Kroeger or anyone else. The only witness we had is dead, and as far as Burke and Muldoon go, there's no way to prove they weren't workin' on their own when they came after me."

"But Muldoon said Randado and Harris would get you, just like they got…"

"Exactly. Got who, Ben? Rangers Lowney, Tompkins, or mebbe Anders? And who shot rancher Peter Hunt, or all of the other victims? Anders did mention Harris and Randado just before he cashed in. My guess is they're responsible for all the killings, but I don't have one shred of proof."

"So we're not gonna ride out to the Cross R?"

"I didn't say that, because that's exactly what I'm plannin' on doin'. If Randado and Harris did kill Anders, they probably don't know I got him out of that building, and that he talked some before he died. I'm gonna try and run a bluff on 'em. First though, I'm gonna mail these papers and the photograph of Lowney's body to

Captain Blawcyzk. I want them safely in the captain's hands just in case anythin' happens to me."

"You mean like a bullet in the back?" Ben questioned.

"Yeah, like a bullet in the back or a knife in the guts."

"You want me to ride along with you?" Ben asked. "You'll be outnumbered at least four to one."

"I've bucked worse. Besides, the Cross R is out of your jurisdiction. You're strictly a town marshal."

"But a Texas Ranger can deputize," Ben reminded him. "I can at least cover your back."

"I can't argue with that," Cody conceded. "As long as you're willing, let's ride."

8

After two hours of steady riding, the Ranger and deputy neared the foothills of the Glass Mountains.

"The Cross R's just beyond that low ridge ahead," Ben told Cody. "As I recollect, there's not much cover between the top of the ridge and the ranch buildings."

"We'll take a look before we ride on in and get an idea what we'll be up against," Cody answered.

Cody touched his spurs to Yankee's flanks to heel the paint into a slow trot. Ben followed close behind on his grulla gelding. Just before the summit of the ridge they reined in their horses and dropped from their saddles. Cody ground-hitched Yankee, while Ben tied his grulla to a stunted live oak. Cody took field glasses from his saddlebags and the lawmen carefully worked their way to the top of the ridge. They dropped to their bellies and crawled the last few feet.

Lying flat on his stomach, Cody lifted the field glasses to his eyes and cautiously shielded the lenses. He studied the barren wind-swept grounds of the Cross R for quite some time before lowering the glasses.

"You were right, Ben," Cody told the deputy. "Except for the fences and a couple of woodpiles, there's absolutely no cover once we top this rise."

The Ranger's careful scrutiny revealed only a few scrawny, drought-shriveled mesquite bushes and cactus. Not enough cover to hide a man, let alone conceal a horse and rider. The only sign of life on the ranch was two cowboys working on a fence.

"What're we gonna do now?" Ben questioned.

"Just what we set out to do, go down there and arrest Monte Harris and Jorge Randado," Cody replied.

He dug his badge out of his shirt pocket and pinned it to his vest.

"We might be ridin' straight into a trap," Ben protested.

"There's not much we can do about that, except spring it."

*   *   *

"We're a couple of mighty clear targets, Ranger. You reckon we're bein' watched?" Ben asked.

They descended the ridge to cross the last several hundred yards before reaching the Cross R.

"You can bet a hat on it," Cody answered.

He pointed out one of the cowboys as the man ducked into the main house.

"If they planned on shootin' us, they would have started by now."

Nonetheless, Cody's stomach muscles tightened at the thought of hot lead ripping through him.

"I sure wish I knew where the other one went," Cody muttered under his breath.

The second man was nowhere in sight. Cody pushed his horse into a trot.

"Remember, Ben, you're to keep an eye on the bunkhouse once we're on the porch. There's not many horses around, so it doesn't appear anyone's in there, but we've gotta be sure."

"You can count on me," Ben confidently replied.

"I know that, or I wouldn't have let you side me."

The man who disappeared into the house reappeared on the porch, rifle in hand.

"Told you they're not ready to start shootin'…at least not yet," Cody said.

"That sure makes me feel a heap better," Ben replied.

A moment later the lawmen rode up in front of the main house, dismounted, and looped their horses' reins over the rail.

"You two lookin' for something?" the man on the porch challenged.

"I'm Earl Dixon, *segundo* here."

"Not something, someone. I'm Texas Ranger Cody Havlicek, and this is Deputy Marshal Ben Tate. I'd like to talk with Monte Harris and Jorge Randado. They here?"

Cody's left hand hovered over the butt of his Colt.

"Mebbe they is, and mebbe they ain't," Dixon snarled.

He spat a thick stream of tobacco juice directly into the dirt between Havlicek's feet as he nodded at the door.

"You'll have to see the boss. He's inside."

"I will."

"Don't reckon I can stop you, seein' as you're wearin' them badges," Dixon replied, waving his rifle toward the entry.

"Right hospitable of you," Cody answered. "By the way, Dixon, you might want to be more careful where you spit out your chaw."

Dixon reddened with anger but said nothing, unable to meet the steady gaze of the Ranger's blue eyes. He merely pushed open the door with the barrel of his rifle.

"Go on in."

"You first," Cody said. "Somethin' about a loaded rifle pointed at my back makes me nervous."

"Suit yourself," Dixon grunted and stepped into the house.

"Ben, you keep an eye on things out here," Cody said.

He followed Dixon inside.

The deputy went to his horse, pulled his rifle from its scabbard, and took a position on the porch.

"Texas Ranger wants to talk to you, boss," Dixon announced as he and Cody stepped into the kitchen.

"I can see that. His badge is blindin' me," Ned Riley grumbled.

"You must be Havlicek. I've been wantin' to meet the hombre who could outdraw Luke Rafferty."

"Well, you've met him," Cody snapped. "That's enough small talk. Where's Monte Harris and Jorge Randado?"

"What possible interest could you have in them?"

"Last night two of your men, Zeke Muldoon and Logan Burke, tried to knife me. I got them first. At about the same time someone caved in Josiah Anders' skull and set fire to his shop."

"And you're implying exactly what, Ranger? I have no idea why Zeke and Logan would try to kill you…if, in fact, they did. Are you sayin' they're also responsible for killin' the photographer?"

"No, I'm only sayin' I want to talk with Harris and Randado about that. Now either tell me where they are, or I'll take this place apart."

"There's no need to get hostile," Riley replied.

"Monte! Jorge! Come in here a minute."

Havlicek's hand automatically went to his Colt. He lifted the gun from its holster as the two men stepped into the room.

"Ranger, that's not really necessary," Riley protested.

"I just feel better havin' my gun ready when I'm in the midst of a pack of coyotes," Cody retorted. "Any one of you makes a false move, my first slug goes into *your* belly, Riley."

"Alright, you've warned me," Riley shrugged.

"Monte, the Ranger here seems to think you and Jorge had somethin' to do with a killin' in town last night. I was tryin' to tell him you were both here all night, but he insisted on talkin' to you himself."

"Ned's right," Harris explained. "Jorge, me, and Earl played poker until way after midnight. Ain't that so, Jorge?"

"It sure is," Randado concurred. "We don't know anythin' about that photographer bein' killed. Don't know nothin' about how his shop caught fire, either."

"That's funny," Cody challenged. "Just before he cashed in his chips, Muldoon said you're involved. An hombre who's gut-shot usually wants to do some talkin' before he goes, and Muldoon did just that. Plus, I dragged Anders out of the fire still alive."

He stopped as he caught a slight movement from the corner of his eye.

"Don't even think about it, Dixon," Cody warned as the Cross R *segundo* started to lift his rifle.

"In fact, why don't all of you boys, nice and easy-like, unbuckle your gunbelts, one-handed, and drop 'em to the floor. Then kick 'em over to me. Right now."

Cody thumbed back the hammer of his Colt for emphasis.

"Do what the Ranger says, men." Riley grumbled and started to unbuckle his gunbelt.

Muttering curses, all four men followed suit.

"Riley, you'd best call your other skunk out of the woodpile, and invite him to join the party too," Cody added.

Riley started to protest, then shrugged in resignation.

"Pete, get in here," he called.

A young cowboy entered from the other room, his hand hovering over the gun on his right hip.

"Drop your gunbelt, Pete. Kick it over with the others, then stand by your boss," Cody ordered.

"Do what the Ranger says, Pete, or he's liable to plug me," Riley emphasized.

The cowboy glanced questioningly at him. Scowling, the man unbuckled and let the gunbelt fall.

"That's much more sociable," Cody drawled.

The last of the weapons he kicked under the table.

"Now to finish my story, Anders talked before he died. He told me Harris and Randado hit him over the head, then set fire to his shop."

"That's impossible," Riley protested. "My men, all of 'em, were right here at the ranch all night."

"Then how do you explain Burke and Muldoon lyin' at the undertaker's with my slugs in 'em?" Cody shot back. "And like I said, Muldoon told me Harris and Randado had gotten Anders."

Cody looked at each man in the room and, as he did, the barrel of his pistol followed the track of his eyes.

"In fact, I've got a few questions for you, Riley. About Chance Lowney's bushwhackin' and the other killin's that have happened down this way...not to mention what happened to Hap Tompkins. He's another Ranger who was sent down here after Lowney was killed, but never showed up."

Cody paused as outside the door Yankee whinnied piercingly, then snorted.

"Ben, is everythin' all right out there?" Cody called, not taking his eyes off his captives.

"Ben?" he repeated.

The door sprang inward to reveal the deputy standing in the entryway, a puzzled expression on his face. Cody glanced at him from the corner of his eye.

"Sorry, Cody," Ben murmured.

Ben's rifle spilled from his hands as he pitched face-down to the floor. A knife was buried to the hilt between his shoulder blades.

"Drop your gun, Ranger, and reach for the ceiling, unless you'd like a bullet in your spine right now!"

For the briefest of moments, Cody considered whirling and dropping to the floor and squeezing off a shot or two. He gave up the idea, lowered the hammer of his Colt, and let it fall.

"Good thing the boss wanted me to check on things down here," Slade Hanscom growled.

He stepped over Ben's body and pulled Cody's Bowie from its sheath and tossed it aside.

"Hand me your rifle, Dixon," Hanscom ordered.

"Sure, Slade. With pleasure."

Dixon grinned cruelly as he retrieved his Winchester from under the table and handed it to Hanscom.

Hanscom reversed the rifle and drove the butt deep into Cody's belly. The Ranger bent over and began retching. Hanscom brought the rifle downward in a vicious arc and the butt hit the back of the Ranger's skull. Cody saw the floor rising to meet him. Waves of pain exploded in his brain. There was a distant thud and darkness.

9

Cody awoke to a pounding agony in his skull and a dull ache in his gut. His mouth was dry as flannel. As his senses returned, he realized he was lying on his side, trussed hand and foot. The dim light of a single lamp indicated night had fallen. He had been unconscious for hours.

Cody tested the ropes binding his wrists and ankles. He winced in pain as the tough rawhide bit into his flesh.

"I've got a snowball's chance in the desert of wigglin' out of these ropes," he murmured. "Whoever tied me up sure knew what he was doin'."

Cody opened his eyes to a squint. Ned Riley stalked over to him, hunkered alongside the Ranger, and studied him carefully.

"Slade, this hombre's awake," Riley announced.

"About time," Hanscom muttered.

He pushed away from a table and joined Riley.

"C'mon, Havlicek, time to get up," he snarled, kicking Cody viciously in the ribs. "Quit playin' possum."

Cody grunted and rolled onto his back. Hanscom drove the heel of his boot into Cody's chest.

"Don't you recognize me, Ranger?" Hanscom sneered.

Cody shook his head in a futile attempt to pierce the fog clouding his vision.

"Slade Hanscom," Cody said.

The Ranger gritted his teeth against the pain.

"Surprised to see me, Havlicek?" Hanscom taunted as he

delivered another kick to Cody's ribs.

"Gotta…admit it," Cody gasped. "Last…I'd heard you…were still in…New Mexico Territory."

"That shows just how stupid you Rangers really are," Hanscom laughed harshly. "I've been bidin' my time, waitin' for the day I could get even with your outfit…ever since the Governor rejected my promotion."

"What promotion? You were never more than a clerk in the Adjutant General's office."

"I was supposed to be Assistant AG," Hanscom shouted.

Infuriated, he kicked Havlicek once again. Cody rolled onto his side, nauseated from the blow.

"That promotion was all set until Jim Blawcyzk dug up those old charges on my war record. Instead of being promoted, I was fired in disgrace. I swore I'd get even."

"You're not smart enough to have pulled off all the killin's that brought the Rangers down here," Cody taunted.

"You may be right, Havlicek," Hanscom said. "But, the man I work for is. He's paid me very well to inform him whenever a Texas Ranger rides into Brewster County."

"I don't suppose you'd care to tell me who that is?"

"It couldn't hurt, I guess, since you'll be dead before noon. But, I won't allow you the satisfaction. You'll go to your grave wonderin'."

Hanscom kicked the Ranger again.

"It's gonna be light soon. Ned, untie his legs and stand him up," Hanscom ordered Riley. "Watch him close. He's tricky as a rattler."

"Yeah, but his fangs have been pulled," Riley laughed.

"Get him movin' and don't take any chances."

Ned Riley slashed the ropes binding Cody's ankles and pulled him to his feet. Needles of pain stabbed through the Ranger's legs as his circulation returned.

"Get him outside and on his horse," Hanscom ordered.

Riley and Pete Sloan dragged the still-wobbly Havlicek onto the porch, where Yankee waited at the rail. Ben Tate's grulla was nowhere in sight. Cody's big paint whickered at his rider.

"Just a small reminder, Havlicek," Hanscom warned. "Don't forget, I know all about that horse of yours. If you have him try anything, I'll put a bullet in his head."

Yankee nervously pawed the ground.

"Easy, pard, everythin's all right," Cody assured his gelding.

"Get up there," Hanscom ordered.

Cody sagged against Yankee's ribs for a moment, then struggled into the saddle. His hands were tied to the horn and his feet to the stirrups. Monte Harris and Jorge Randado emerged from the barn, leading six horses.

Riley tied a lead to Yankee's bridle and the paint snapped viciously at the Cross R foreman. Yankee twisted his neck to look back at his rider, his liquid brown eyes rolling in anger and confusion.

"Just relax, pal."

Cody tried to calm his mount while Riley wrapped Yankee's reins around the Ranger's saddlehorn. Still half-dazed and sick to his stomach, the lawman slumped in the saddle. Riley took the lead and yanked the horse forward. The six outlaws mounted up.

"Enjoy that sunrise. It'll be the last one you ever see, Havlicek," said Riley.

The outlaws laughed as they rode away from the Cross R and the sun burst blood-red and golden over the eastern horizon.

Cody sagged painfully in his saddle. With every jarring hoofbeat, he replayed the confrontation at the Cross R. Cody keenly felt the loss of the affable young deputy. He mumbled incoherently to himself.

"Just keep your mouth shut, Ranger," Riley snarled.

"Let him talk as much as he wants, Ned," Hanscom laughed. "He won't be doin' much of it after today."

The Ranger slipped back into morose silence.

You'd best stop worryin' and try to figure a way out of this, Cody thought.

*   *   *

Shortly before noon, Hanscom ordered a halt. The men reined in their horses and dropped from their saddles.

"This is the end of the line for you, Havlicek," Hanscom announced. "Monte, Jorge, get him off his horse. Don't trust Havlicek or that devil of a bronc."

Harris slashed the ropes that held Cody in the saddle and Randado shoved him from Yankee's back. The Ranger grunted in pain as he tumbled to the ground. He landed heavily.

"Get him up. We're wastin' time," Hanscom snapped.

Randado dragged Cody to his feet.

Hanscom laughed viciously as he leveled his pistol at Yankee's head.

"You won't be needin' this horse anymore, Havlicek, and I'm not takin' any chances with him."

"G'wan, Yank! Get outta here!" Cody shouted.

Instantly the paint whirled around and streaked across the gully-slashed landscape. He squealed in pain as Hanscom's hastily fired bullet tore along his flank. The big gelding swerved sharply and disappeared into a brush-choked ravine. Cody sighed with relief as his horse disappeared.

"Blast it!" Hanscom cursed. "I missed him."

"You want a couple of us to go after him, Slade?" Randado asked.

"No, don't waste your time. It'd be no use. You wouldn't ever get within rifle range of that four-legged beast."

Hanscom turned back to Cody.

"You're not gonna get away so easy, Havlicek. Head over that way."

Hanscom rammed the barrel of Cody's own rifle into the Ranger's back and sent him stumbling toward the rim of a deep canyon.

"Now you've got two choices," Hanscom snarled as Cody reached the edge of the precipice. "Either you can jump, or I'll put a bullet in your back and dump you into the canyon. It doesn't matter to me which one you choose. Either way you will be just as dead. And *you* can bet a hat on that."

"Wrong, Hanscom," said Cody.

The Ranger turned to face his captors.

"I've got a third choice. If you're gonna kill me, you'll have to do it from the front, lookin' right at me."

"My pleasure, Havlicek."

Hanscom leveled Cody's Winchester at the Ranger's middle and pulled the trigger. Cody recoiled at the impact of the heavy slug smashing into his belly. It propelled him backward. He teetered at the brink of the cliff for just a moment, then plummeted over the edge.

"Guess that takes care of one more cussed Ranger," Earl Dixon sneered.

"Lucky for all of us I spotted Ben Tate on the porch and he thought I was his friend," said Hanscom. "If I hadn't come along, our whole deal would've been ruined."

"We could'a handled that Ranger," Ned Riley objected.

"Not until I showed up."

10

A solitary buzzard circled slowly downward toward the figure sprawled on the rocks below. The winged scavenger dropped ever closer to the motionless man. Suddenly, it rose back into the sky, squawking in frustration as its meal rolled onto its back.

The ugly bird's protests pierced Cody Havlicek's fogged brain. He drifted back to consciousness. His eyes flickered open. The half-dazed Ranger recoiled in horror at a leering skull only inches from his face. He scrambled frantically away on his hands and knees from the stark vision. His heart pounded and guts churned as he stopped short from plummeting over a five hundred foot cliff. Cold sweat beaded Cody's forehead as he heard several rocks dislodge and smash to the canyon below. Still dizzy, Cody edged away from the sheer drop.

"Better take it easy for a few minutes," Cody warned himself.

He took stock of his injuries. His shirt was in tatters, his jeans ripped, and his Stetson had disappeared. Cody's body was a mass of scrapes and bruises. He managed a grim chuckle as he glanced down at his belt buckle. It was badly dented by Slade Hanscom's bullet. An inch higher and he would have died with an ounce of lead buried deep in his guts.

"I guess the good Lord isn't ready for me quite yet," he muttered.

He took a quick look around his precarious perch.

"Course, if I don't find a way out of this fix, I might end up wishin' Hanscom had plugged me. Dying of thirst and starving to death is not a better way to go."

Taking a deep breath, Cody managed to pull himself upright, swaying only slightly.

"Don't seem to be any bones broken," he noted with satisfaction.

His gaze ran over the narrow shelf where he'd landed. He had fallen upon thick clumps of mesquite which had broken his fall. Cody shuddered once again as he looked at the grinning skull and bleached bones—the broken remains of a once living, breathing, human being.

Cody limped over to the skeleton. Torn and faded shirt and jeans were still draped over the bones. An empty gunbelt encircled the waist and scuffed boots still encased the feet. What caught Cody's eyes; however, and brought an exclamation of rage to his lips, was the silver star on silver circle pinned to the cracked leather vest the skeleton wore.

"Hap Tompkins!" Cody exclaimed.

He knelt alongside the missing Ranger's remains. He studied a ragged hole in Tompkins' shirt, which was surrounded by a faint brownish stain. With trembling hand, Cody pulled open the shirt to reveal a bullet-shattered breastbone.

"At least you died quick and clean, Hap," he whispered, "not like I'm gonna cash in."

Shakily, Cody stood back up and examined the place where he'd landed.

Havlicek stalked along the shelf, the hopelessness of his situation quickly becoming apparent. Above him was a sheer red rock wall, thirty feet high. A few scraggly bushes clung precariously to the rocks, none of them substantial enough to hold his weight. The few crevices that broke the face of the wall failed to provide enough handholds for him to scale the cliff. The shelf where he stood was only about twenty feet in length, one end curling back into the rock wall, the other breaking off sharply in a long drop to the canyon floor. Worse, the shelf slanted downward, inducing a feeling of vertigo.

"There's not even enough loose rocks here to bury what's left of poor, Hap," Cody said.

Wearily, he slumped against the wall, pulling off his bandanna to wipe sweat from his forehead.

The sun passed its zenith and the full force of its blistering heat beat down into the canyon. It radiated off the sun-blasted rocks and turned the shelf into a virtual oven. With no Stetson, Cody's face and head were unprotected from the merciless rays. His lips were beginning to swell and blister. He crawled behind a stunted redberry juniper, utilizing its scant shelter.

"Dunno how long I can hold out," Cody mumbled. "Sure hope I pass out before I go mad from thirst or the heat. If I last a couple more hours, mebbe I can make it 'til mornin'."

He glanced up at the sky and placed a few pebbles in his mouth. He closed his eyes against the blinding sunlight. A horse's whinny, sharp and inquiring, drifted over the canyon's rim.

"Yankee?"

Cody scrambled to his feet, shielding his eyes as he gazed upward.

"Yankee!" he shouted again.

An answering whinny came to his ears. The gelding's muzzle showed visibly over the rim of the canyon as the horse sought his master.

"Stay back, Yank!"

His paint pawed at the edge of the cliff and the horse's hooves sent several loose rocks tumbling over. The last thing the Ranger needed was for his friend to come crashing down on him.

Cody stared up in frustration. The sixty-foot length of catch rope on his saddle would be more than long enough to reach him and haul him out of his rocky deathtrap. However, as intelligent as Yankee was, he sure wasn't going to untie that rope—or dally one end around the saddlehorn, and toss the other to his rider. Cody's horse and lariat might as well be on the moon.

Yankee whinned frantically and pawed at the dirt once again. More rocks tumbled over the cliff's edge shattering at Cody's feet.

"Get outta here, boy! Git...now, Yank!" Cody ordered.

With a defiant snort, Yankee turned and was gone.

Once his horse vanished, Cody sank into despair as he lay back against the rocks.

"You're the lucky one, Hap," he said with a glance at Tompkins' bleached bones.

He pushed himself unsteadily to his feet and stumbled toward the jagged edge of the shelf. He reached the rim of his perilous perch and halted. Quivering with anger, he looked into the depths of the canyon and at the thin ribbon of blue that marked the creek bed far below. The Ranger stared down and gradually backed away from the edge.

"You're not gonna give in," Cody sternly told himself. "The sun'll be goin' down in a couple of hours and it'll cool off quick. Tomorrow, you're gonna find a way off this cliff."

He staggered back to the meager shelter of the juniper. Cody stretched out under the bush. Exhaustion finally claimed him and he fell into a fitful sleep.

When the Ranger awoke, darkness had overtaken the sky, and a full moon shone brightly. After the blazing heat of the day, Cody now shivered from the chill of a desert night.

"I've gotta make a fire," he thought, reaching into his shirt pocket, "or it's gonna be mighty chilly. A fire! That's it. Mebbe someone'll see it from up above."

He dug frantically in his pockets.

"Matches…my matches have gotta be here somewhere."

It was only a matter of moments before Cody realized his matches were lost. Even if they were lying somewhere on the shelf, there was no way to find them until daylight.

"Well, it was a thought anyway," he muttered.

He hunkered against the wall to soak in the day's heat which radiated from the still warm rocks. Cody glanced at Hap Tompkins' bones, which glowed eerily luminescent in the moonlight.

"How about it, Hap?" Cody called to the skeleton. "You got any idea what this is all about, or'd they get you before you even had a chance to start diggin' around?"

With a sigh, Cody huddled closer to the wall.

The night wore on, occasionally punctuated by the howling of a wolf or coyote, or the scream of a hunting cougar. Despair again started eating away at the Ranger. His attempts at prayer failed to ease his mind. His throat felt parched and hunger gnawed at his belly.

"You've got to get your mind on somethin' else," Cody grimly warned himself. "You'd best start tryin' to put the pieces of this puzzle together."

Lying with his back against the cliff, Cody began reviewing the little he'd learned so far.

"Let's see. There's been a harness maker killed, then a Mexican freighter, and a feed store owner, not to mention the biggest rancher in these parts. I'd bet my last dollar Lem Tucker didn't get killed by fallin' off his horse, neither. Guaranteed he was murdered. Cap'n Blawcyzk sends two veteran Rangers down here, and both of 'em wind up dead."

Cody frowned, deep in thought.

"Now, Chance and Hap were killed simply because they were doin' their job. But how about the others? There's got to be some connection, but what is it? I sure wish Anders could've told me somethin' more before he died. How's Kroeger, the newspaperman, tie in with all of this? And who's his pardner?"

Cody gazed up at the stars, now dimming as dawn neared.

"Doesn't any of it matter if I don't figure a way outta here. And if I'm gonna do that, I'd better try to get a little more shut-eye. Lord, I'd sure appreciate it if you could show me the way."

The Ranger curled up on his side, trying his best to ignore the chill seeping into his bones. Sleep was slow to come as Cody kept turning over the pieces of the puzzle in his mind.

*   *   *

Despite hunger and thirst, the cold of the desert night, and the nagging questions in his head, Cody finally did manage to catch a few more hours of sleep. He awakened shortly after sunup

"Good mornin', Hap," he croaked through his cracked, swollen lips. "Today's the day I say *adios* to you, *compadre*."

Painstakingly, Cody began surveying every inch of the wall above him. He checked crevices and tested shrubs clinging to the rocks. He hoped to find some foothold that would at least start his upward climb. All too soon; however, it was apparent there was no way up that cliff. Cody was trapped as effectively as if he were locked in a dungeon.

"Appears like I'll be stayin' with you for good, Hap," Cody muttered to Tompkins' remains. "I guess I would've been better off if Hanscom had plugged me. Too bad his aim wasn't a bit better."

"I'm sorry, Sarah," Cody whispered. "I never thought it'd end like this. You never knowin' what happened to me. Looks like those pictures Anders took will be all you have."

The day wore endlessly on. The blistering heat tormented the trapped Ranger. Yankee's insistent whinny again pierced the depths of the canyon and the horse's muzzle appeared overhead. Cody ordered him back once again. The big gelding remained at the edge of the cliff for some time, then turned away. Once he was gone, Cody crawled behind the juniper, seeking out the slightest bit of shade.

By that afternoon, Cody's lips were puffed and blackened. His tongue swelled and protruded from between cracked lips. His face and neck were painfully burned and the backs of his hands blistered. Hallucinations taunted him. He saw pools of cool, clear water, surrounded by green meadows and towering shade trees. Several times he found himself stumbling blindly toward the visions. Once he stopped at the very edge of the shelf and the illusions disappeared like smoke.

Night fell, the cool air brought relief to the Ranger's tortured body. Cody crawled from behind the juniper and fixed his gaze on Hap Tompkins' skeleton.

"Reckon I can last a couple more days at best, ol' pard," he told the bones. "Then I'll be ridin' with you and Chance Lowney across the Lord's green pastures. If he'll have me."

Cody dropped to his knees, gazed up at the sky as it faded to deep indigo and stars began to prick the heavens.

"Lord, I know I ain't been one of the best of men," he prayed. "And it looks like I won't be gettin' to church anytime soon. But, Lord, I'd appreciate it if you'd see to it that Sarah and my children are taken care of. I don't know what I ever did to deserve them. And, I'd be obliged if you could look after Yank. Thanks."

Resigned to his fate, Cody stared up at the star-studded sky, until sleep again claimed him.

*   *   *

Cody was jolted out of his slumber by a blinding flash and a tremendous crack of thunder. A bolt of lightning struck a cedar on the opposite rim of the canyon. The shattered tree toppled, trailing sparks and flame.

Jagged bolts of lightning rent the scudding clouds overhead, while thunder rumbled threateningly. A few drops of rain spattered on the rocks, quickly turning into a torrential downpour. The wind howled through the canyon and whipped the tattered remnants of Cody's clothing.

He huddled miserably against the wall, trying to shield himself from the wind-driven rain and hail. At the same time, he lifted his head and opened his mouth to swallow as much water as possible. Every raindrop or hailstone which struck his sun-ravaged skin bit like a hornet's sting. With each lightning bolt, Hap Tompkins' skeleton seemed to come to life, the skull leered tauntingly at him.

"I sure hope Yank took off and got to shelter. I'd hate to think he got hurt. Mebbe he'll finally give up on me. This might turn out for the best."

Thoroughly drenched and chilled to the bone, Cody sagged to his side. He drank as much liquid as he could and shivered violently as the deluge continued.

11

Tommy Mashburn was awakened by the low rumbling of voices in the front office of the Alpine Advisor.

"Holy smokes, Joe's gonna wonder where the heck I am!" he exclaimed.

After returning from delivering the week's issue, Tommy had sat down in the back room for a moment's rest. He had fallen asleep.

"Lucky for me Mr. Kroeger is still here, or I'd be locked in all night. I hope Joe's still got supper waitin' for me."

Tommy froze as he placed his hand on the doorknob. He heard Al Kroeger raise his voice in anger.

"Are you sure no one saw you come here?" the newspaperman demanded of someone in the front room.

"I'm positive."

Tommy recognized Slade Hanscom's voice.

"Is that boy you've got workin' for you around here anywhere? It wouldn't do to have him hear us."

"No," Kroeger assured him. "He finished up an hour ago and left. I don't need him again until Monday. He's still bunkin' at the livery stable, so we don't have to worry about him. Now Slade, you'd better have some good news for me."

"I do." Hanscom grinned triumphantly. "We don't have to worry about that Ranger anymore."

"You took care of Havlicek?"

"I sure did," Hanscom boasted. "He's lyin' gut-shot at the bottom of Blue Canyon. With any luck, he took a long time to die. Ben Tate, that meddlin' deputy, is finished too. We also had to get rid of Anders. Cody Havlicek'd been talking to him, but I don't think he got much. Jorge and Monte burned Anders' shop, so his death looks like an accident."

"Good work, Slade. Anders knew too much anyway. What about that big paint gelding of Havlicek's? I'd sure like to own that fine piece of horseflesh."

"I had to shoot that devil. Like I told you before, that paint was a one man horse. He'd kill anyone who tried to ride him, except the Ranger. You couldn't chance ridin' a dead Ranger's mount anyway."

"I guess you're right at that. It's best that horse disappears."

"Cody!" The name slipped softly from Tommy's lips as he recognized Hanscom's description of the Ranger's horse. "He's a Texas Ranger. I knew he wasn't an outlaw."

The boy's mind raced at his discovery. He barely heard Kroeger's next question over the pounding of his heart.

"How about the rest of our plans? Is everything set?"

"Riley and his men will be in town by mornin'. Mark Carlisle's being taken care of too."

"Excellent. I'll have to talk with Silas, since he's the mayor. I can persuade him and the town council to appoint Riley the new sheriff once Carlisle's dead. It shouldn't be too hard to convince folks we need a tougher man in office. Especially since the Texas Rangers haven't been able to stop crime in Brewster County."

Kroeger paused in thought for a moment.

"Slade, why don't we spread the word that Havlicek, or Jim Smith as he was calling himself, was in fact an outlaw on the run, not a lawman. We could say he'd killed a real Ranger and stole his badge. Ben Tate figured that out and tried to arrest Havlicek, but got himself killed. Maybe we can also say Havlicek gunned down Carlisle and disappeared into Mexico."

"That sounds like a fine idea, Al, especially if you print that story in your paper," Slade agreed.

Not waiting to hear anything more, Tommy cautiously edged away from the door.

I've gotta help Cody, he thought.

The boy slipped out the back door of the newspaper office, into the alleyway, and broke into a run.

"Tommy! Where in blazes have you been?" Joe questioned as the youngster burst into the stable. "I've been keepin' the stew warm for you."

"There's no time to eat right now," Tommy breathlessly answered.

He pulled bridle, saddle, and blanket from a peg, raced into Brownie's stall, and saddled the mare.

"Joe, tell me how to find Blue Canyon."

"Blue Canyon?" Joe echoed. "There's nothin' out there but scrub brush and rattlesnakes. Why're you in such an all-fired hurry to go to Blue Canyon?"

"Cody's out there. He's in trouble. He's a Texas Ranger, not an outlaw. Slade Hanscom shot him. He killed Cody's horse, too. I've got to try and help him."

"Cody?" Joe rubbed his jaw in puzzlement.

"Yeah. The tall feller I rode in with."

"Jim, uh, Cody Smith's a Texas Ranger?"

"Yeah, only his name's not Smith. I heard Mr. Kroeger and Mr. Hanscom talkin' about shootin' him, and killin' a deputy and somebody else. They're gonna kill Sheriff Carlisle, too."

Tommy's voice broke.

"Joe, you've gotta help me."

"Whoa, easy pardner," Joe urged. "You'd better go slow, and start at the beginnin'. You sure about all this?"

"I overheard everythin' from the back room," Tommy insisted as he tightened the cinch. "Mr. Hanscom said he'd gut-shot Cody and left him to die at the bottom of Blue Canyon. I've got to try and find him."

Joe thumbed back his battered hat and scratched his head.

"We'd better not take any chances," he decided. "I'll warn Mark Carlisle while you head for Blue Canyon and see if you can find the Ranger."

"But how do I get there?" Tommy interrupted.

"Hold on a second and let me finish," Joe replied. "Take the road east to Marathon about six miles. You'll see a big split rock. A trail branches off to the right. Take it about two miles further to where the trail forks. You want to take the left fork. It leads straight to the edge of Blue Canyon.

"That's quite a bit of ground to cover," said Joe. "You've got no idea where to look for Cody. You've got to realize that Ranger could be dead."

"I know," the boy hesitated. "But he patched me up and got Brownie back. I'm not gonna leave him lyin' out there for the coyotes and buzzards. If Cody's in Blue Canyon, I'll find him."

"Y'know, kid, I believe you will," Joe nodded.

Tommy climbed onto his saddle.

"Hold on a minute," Joe said. "You'll need water and grub. If the Ranger is still alive, he'll sure be needin' some too. I'll get you somethin—oh, and you'll likely need rope. Grab that off the wall."

Joe ducked into his office and a few minutes later emerged with a full canteen, a packet of jerky, and hardtack. He handed them to Tommy. Sliding the stable's rear door, Joe checked the alleyway.

"All clear. Take it easy until you get out of town so nobody gets suspicious. It's kinda cloudy out there, so there's not much of a moon. You'll be travelin' in full dark. It'll probably be best if you ride for a few miles and hole up. You don't want to chance missin' the turnoff. And don't get caught out in the open durin' a gullywasher."

"All right," Tommy agreed. "I'll do what you say. You'd better watch yourself too."

"Don't fret. The sheriff will know what to do. G'wan, get outta here before somebody comes by."

Tommy heeled Brownie into a shuffling walk and disappeared into the dark.

"Cody Smith, or Jim Smith, or whatever his name is, a Texas Ranger," Joe thought.

He watched for movement in the alley.

"Huh. Never would've guessed it. Shame about that Yankee horse of his, too. That paint was one mean son of a gun, but he was some cayuse. Best one I've ever seen in these parts."

Joe left the stable and crossed the street to the sheriff's office.

"Appears I'm in luck," he muttered, observing the dim light from the windows. "Looks like he hasn't started his rounds yet."

"Mark!" the hostler called as he pushed open the door. "Mark!"

The sheriff lay slumped over his desk with a dark crimson blotch staining the back of his shirt. Joe stepped into the cramped room. A muffled pop of a Derringer exploded from the shadows. The hostler staggered from the impact of a .41 caliber slug hitting him in the chest. The bullet spun Joe around and slammed him against the wall. He slid to the floor and moaned once as he tried to push himself up. Joe lay unmoving. The hidden gunman stepped over him, closed the office door, and walked unhurriedly down the street.

Once the door shut, Joe lifted his head and dragged himself across the floor. His voice failed him as he tried to call for help. He managed to crawl as far as the door and attempted to pull himself up and reach the knob. His strength ebbing, Joe dropped back. His fingernails scratched a shallow track in the heavy oak door. With a long sigh, the hostler rolled onto his back and lay still.

12

"I never thought the sun would feel good again," Cody sighed.

He rolled painfully away from the sheltering juniper. Sometime during the night the violent storm had played itself out. Once the rain abated he'd drifted back to sleep. Now as the sun rose, its warmth began to dry his clothes. Cody gazed through his swollen, narrowed eyelids, noting with blurred vision that Hap Tompkins' skeleton still reposed on the shelf.

"Water!" Cody exclaimed.

He did not get enough the night before. The storm had filled several depressions in the rock with the life-giving fluid. He hobbled to the nearest one and flung himself on his belly. He drank and the liquid soothed his parched lips and throat. He went to each depression and greedily sucked down the contents.

"Better take it easy," the Ranger warned himself.

He pushed forcefully back from the shallow pool and glanced over at the skeleton.

"Hap's sure not gonna want any. Sorry, pardner," he apologized to the bones.

Cody sighed in frustration as he realized the water he'd just drunk would only prolong his agony, not end it. Already the hot rays of the sun were drying up the shallow puddles. Several had evaporated to mere damp spots on the rock. By noon the water would be nothing but a bitter memory.

As the day wore on, with the sun again beating down on Havlicek, his hallucinations returned more vivid and lifelike than ever. Images of blue water and green plants appeared on the canyon's rim, only to vanish as Cody stumbled toward them. When Yankee's whinny once again rang across the canyon, the Ranger was convinced it was just another trick of his tormented mind. The horse's frantic pawing sent several loose rocks tumbling over the edge. They crashed down the ledge where Cody was imprisoned.

"Yankee." Cody's voice was barely a croak. "I told you to get outta here, bud."

His paint continued to paw at the edge of the cliff. Cody struggled to his feet, grabbed a rock, and tossed it weakly toward the top of the wall.

"I said git, Yank!" Cody rasped a shout.

The big gelding responded with yet another inquiring whicker. The Ranger sank wearily against the rocks.

"All right, Yank. Stay if that's what you want, you stubborn ol' cayuse," Cody muttered.

The Ranger was comforted by Yankee's presence, as well as relieved to know the horse had survived the storm. At least he wouldn't be alone when death finally overtook him. Yankee hovered overhead like some equine guardian angel. Sooner or later the survival instinct would force the gelding to abandon his long-time companion.

Cody moaned and slumped onto his side. His body could endure perhaps one more day of this punishment.

*   *   *

"All right, Andy. I'm comin'," Cody called out as he jerked awake at the sound of his son's voice and looked around in confusion.

"Guess I'm finally becoming delirious," he dejectedly thought. "I could've sworn I heard Andy callin' me."

He sagged back against the rocks, with Yankee's whinnies again ringing in his ears.

"Cody!"

The boy's voice became louder and more insistent. Havlicek staggered to his feet.

"Andy?" he wondered, still puzzled. "What's my boy doin' way out here? Can't be. I'm just imaginin' it."

A wave of dizziness overtook him. He braced himself against the rocks.

"Cody! Where are you?" echoed down the canyon once again.

"Someone is callin' me," Cody dimly realized.

He stumbled away from the wall. Renewed hope surged through his mind as he gazed upward and tried to focus his sun-scorched eyes on the cliff's edge.

"Cody! It's Tommy! Where are you?"

"Tommy?" Cody managed to squeak out. "Tommy! Down here!" he called, slightly louder. "I'm down here!"

"Cody!" Tommy exclaimed as he appeared at the rim of the canyon, with Yankee at his side. "Hold on! I'm gonna get you outta there as quick as I can."

The youngster and horse disappeared and Tommy returned a few moments later. He tossed the end of Cody's lariat down to the trapped Ranger.

"That rope's tied to Yankee's saddle," Tommy shouted. "He'll pull you outta there."

Cody grabbed the rope, grateful Tommy had tied a loop for him. He fumbled for several minutes as his blistered fingers struggled with the lariat. He managed to slip the rope under his arms and tighten it around his chest.

"*Adios*, Hap," he whispered as he took a last sorrowful look at his remains. "I'll try to come back for you once this job is done."

Cody tugged feebly on the rope as a signal he was ready. Tommy urged Yankee to start hauling his companion off the ledge. The big horse leaned forward, his muscles bulged under his sleek hide and his hooves dug into the flinty earth. Steadily Cody rose from his rocky prison.

The lariat cut into his raw, sunburned flesh. Cody miscalculated in his attempts to stay clear of the rock wall and bounced jarringly off of it. It seemed an eternity until the semiconscious Ranger reached the top. Several times, Tommy pulled back on Yankee's bridle to slow the horse's pace.

"Take it easy, Yank. You don't want to hurt Cody more'n he already is," the youth cautioned.

The paint lurched forward against Cody's dead weight. Yankee pulled steadily and the injured Havlicek came over the cliff onto solid ground. Cody sprawled on his back and gasped for breath. Tommy removed the rope and placed a canteen to the Ranger's lips.

"Not too much, Cody," the boy warned.

The Ranger began to gulp down the water.

"All right. Thanks. Thanks, Tommy," Cody croaked.

Yankee nickered and eagerly nuzzled his master's face.

"Easy, Yank," Cody warned his horse. "That hurts too much, pal."

He reached up to rub the paint's velvety muzzle.

"I never thought I'd touch you again, old pard."

Yankee lowered his head and Cody slipped the bridle from over his ears.

"There, that'll feel better," he soothed the horse, then turned to the boy. "Tommy, take his saddle off for me, will you?"

"In a minute. You'd better take a few more sips of water first," Tommy advised.

Cody drank a little more and poured some of the water over his face. Tommy removed the saddle from Yankee's back. The gelding immediately dropped to the ground, rolled in the dust, and shook himself vigorously.

"That sure feels good, doesn't it, Yank?" Cody laughed and passed the canteen back to Tommy.

"Thanks, son," he repeated. "I thought for sure I was a goner. Couldn't have held out much longer. How in the world did you find me?"

"Cody, you'd better rest a bit," Tommy urged. "Lemme help you over to those trees first."

He pointed towards dwarf cottonwoods growing around a small spring.

"I've got some jerky and biscuits in my saddlebags. You'd best try to eat somethin' while we talk. I've got an awful lot to tell you."

"Sounds good," Cody agreed.

Tommy helped him to his feet, sagging under the big Ranger's weight. Cody placed an arm across the boy's shoulders. Supported by the youngster, Cody staggered to the scant shade. Yankee whickered contentedly and followed his every step. The Ranger dropped to his belly to dip his head in an alkaline spring. He sucked in the cool liquid greedily. The bitter water tasted as sweet as molasses. Already, his swollen tongue was beginning to return to its normal size. Refreshed by the drink, his strength increased, Cody stumbled over to one of the cottonwoods and braced himself against its trunk. Yankee nuzzled him at his shoulder. The Ranger spotted the ragged, inflamed bullet slash that marred his horse's right flank. His eyes turned to chips of ice. This was one more thing Slade Hanscom would have to answer for.

"It'll be all right, boy," Cody assured his horse. "I'm gonna patch you up."

He tore a strip from the tattered remnants of his shirt.

"Tommy, will you wet this for me?" he asked.

The boy took the cloth and dipped it in the spring.

"While I'm cleanin' out this bullet slash, I'd sure appreciate it if you'd go to my saddle and dig out that tin of salve."

"Sure thing, Cody."

Havlicek gently washed dirt and dried blood from the wound in Yankee's flank.

"This what you're lookin' for?" Tommy asked, as he passed two tins to the Ranger. "I got that witch hazel for you too."

"That's it. Thanks, son."

He crooned softly to his horse as he doused Yankee's injury with the witch hazel, then carefully coated it with the salve.

"There you go, pard," he told the paint. "In a couple of days, you'll be good as new."

Yankee nuzzled at his hip pocket. Cody chuckled.

"Oh no, you don't. There's no peppermints until we get back to town. I'm fresh out. Sorry, bud, but your candy hasn't been one of my biggest worries the past couple of days. Go get some grass," he ordered the horse, with a gentle slap on his rump.

Yankee snorted, shook his head, and trotted off to join Brownie. Both horses busily cropped the tough buffalo grass alongside the water hole.

"You might want to patch yourself up a little too," Tommy advised. "Some of those scrapes are lookin' pretty raw."

"I reckon you're right."

Cody winced with the effort and coated his wounds with the witch hazel. He covered them with salve. When finished, he sank to the ground and settled in the shade of the cottonwood.

"All right, Tommy," he grimaced. "You said you've got a lot to tell me. You might as well get started."

The boy stared at the badge still pinned to Cody's badly scraped vest and handed him a strip of jerky.

"You really are a Texas Ranger!" he exclaimed.

"Sure am." Cody grinned lopsidedly as he took a bite of the tough, stringy meat. "I couldn't tell you that, though. It would've been too dangerous for you. How'd you figure it out anyway? You still didn't tell me what you're doin' all by yourself way out here."

"I was lookin' for you." Tommy explained. "I was in the back room of the newspaper office when I overheard Mr. Hanscom tell Mr. Kroeger that he'd shot a Texas Ranger. He said he left you with a bullet in your belly at the bottom of Blue Canyon. Then Mr. Kroeger asked about your horse. He wanted Yankee for himself, but Mr. Hanscom said that he'd shot your paint too. Said he was a one man bronc. I recognized Yankee from that description, so I knew the Ranger who'd been shot and left for dead had to be you."

Tommy paused for breath.

"There's more. Mr. Hanscom claimed he'd also killed a deputy and another man."

"The deputy'd be Ben Tate, the marshal over to Marathon," Cody explained.

The Ranger hesitated and took another bite of jerky.

"A couple of Hanscom's men killed a photographer named Anders," continued Cody. "Looks like Al Kroeger is behind all the killin's down here. He's been hidin' behind the cover of being a law and order newspaperman."

"That's not everything," Tommy said. "Mr. Hanscom was also gonna kill Sheriff Carlisle."

"Then we'd best get movin' so I can try and stop him."

Cody attempted to rise, only to fall back against the tree as a wave of nausea overcame him.

"Dunno how far I can ride, but I've got to try. I'll rest a few more minutes while I eat and drink a little more. Then we'll head out."

"We might have time," Tommy tried to convince the Ranger. "I was able to get away without Mr. Kroeger and Mr. Hanscom knowin' I'd been listenin'. I told Joe at the stable what I'd heard, and he went to warn the sheriff. I still didn't know if I'd be able to find you, or even if you were still alive. I'd been searchin' along the rimrock for an hour or so when Brownie heard Yankee whinny. She whinnied back to him. We found him runnin' back and forth and lookin' over the edge of the canyon. I knew you had to be down there. It's sure lucky for you that you landed on that ledge. Yankee let me walk right up to him."

"Mighty grateful, Tommy, but we have to get back there."

"Don't worry about Mr. Kroeger and Mr. Hanscom. Joe and Sheriff Carlisle can handle them."

"Yeah, but they sure can't handle Ned Riley and his bunch of renegades," Cody grunted and took another swallow from the canteen. "Those hombres have already killed two Rangers. What's left of one of 'em is down on that bench. If you hadn't come along when you did, I'd be in the same shape."

"Cody, you're right!" Tommy exclaimed. "I plumb forgot. Mr. Kroeger said somethin' about havin' Ned Riley appointed the new sheriff. Riley and his men are supposed to be ridin' into town today. Mr. Kroeger was also gonna tell folks that you'd killed the deputy and Sheriff Carlisle. His story was gonna be that you were really an outlaw who'd killed a Ranger and stolen his badge."

"Then we've got to get movin'," Havlicek snapped.

Cody forced himself to his feet and stood swaying slightly as he whistled sharply for Yankee. The big gelding lifted his head, whinnied a response, and trotted to the Ranger's side. The horse seemed eager to run again after his days of vigil. Brownie trotted along at his heels.

"Cody, you're in no shape to ride, let alone take on a whole passel of outlaws. And we're more than eight miles from town," Tommy protested.

Havlicek led Yankee to where he'd dropped his saddle and bridle.

"I've got no choice," Cody replied.

The Ranger slipped the bridle over Yankee's ears and slid the bit into his mouth. He placed the blanket and saddle on the horse's back and tightened the cinches. He pulled himself painfully into the saddle, then looked at his empty rifle scabbard.

"Tommy, have you got a gun?"

"Just my old rifle," Tommy answered, as he settled onto Brownie's back.

"That's better'n nothin'. It'll have to do. I'll need to borrow it."

"You're welcome to it, Cody. I've got no spare bullets."

The youngster pulled the ancient Henry from his saddle boot and handed it to the Ranger.

"There's seven shells in the chamber," said Tommy.

"That'll work."

Cody nodded as he checked the action.

"Don't worry," he added, seeing the concerned expression on Tommy's face. "I'll stop those hombres. If I can live through bein' shot in the belly and gettin' knocked off a cliff to roast like a turkey, I'm sure not worried about takin' on a bunch of renegades in a gunfight. And once all this is over, I've also gotta make some things up to you."

"Just don't get yourself killed," Tommy pleaded. "That's all I want."

"Ain't aimin' for that to happen."

Cody grinned and patted the youngster on the back.

"Meanwhile, we've got some miles to cover, and we're wastin' daylight. Let's ride!"

Cody nudged his spurs into Yankee's ribs, sending the big gelding leaping forward at a trot.

13

Cody and Tommy neared the outskirts of Alpine. The lawman was seriously weakened by his exposure to the elements. He now rode slumped over Yankee's neck and clung to the paint's thick mane. The Ranger's injuries had forced them to slow their pace to a steady trot.

"I still say you should see the doc before you take on that bunch of no-good bushwhackers," Tommy insisted.

"There'll be time enough for that after I finish what has to be done," Cody replied, "and don't forget what I told you."

"I know." Tommy heaved a sigh. "Before we reach town, we're gonna split up. I've gotta head for the livery stable, let Joe know I've found you, and we're both to stay put until we hear from you. I still don't understand why I can't help you."

"You already have helped by pullin' me outta that canyon," Cody patiently explained. "The only thing you could do now if you're seen with me is get yourself killed. The hombres I'm after won't stop at pluggin' you just 'cause you're a kid."

He smiled broadly at the boy.

"I can't chance that happenin' to my new pardner," the Ranger said.

"We're pards?" Tommy repeated. "You really mean that, Cody?"

"I wouldn't have said it, if I didn't. If you're ever gonna be a Texas Ranger, you've got to learn to follow orders. So, are you gonna find Joe and stay put?"

"I sure will, Ranger!" Tommy snapped a crisp salute, grinning from ear to ear.

"Good. The town's just ahead. We'll split up once we reach Dry Fork."

*   *   *

"Let's hope we're not already too late, Yank," Cody muttered.

He walked the paint down the alley behind the buildings on Alpine's main street and turned into the narrow alleyway alongside the sheriff's office.

"This wind'll help some," he remarked.

A fitful gust ruffled Yankee's mane. The gentle breeze that had been blowing all day was now steadily increasing, helping to muffle the horse's hoofbeats.

"You stay here, and make sure you keep quiet," the Ranger warned the gelding, with a soft pat to his muzzle. "I can't have anyone spottin' you before I figure out the lay of the land."

Cody looped his reins over the saddlehorn and slid Tommy's rifle from the scabbard before he stepped carefully around the corner. Several passersby stared curiously at the rifle-toting, hatless, sun-blistered figure who wore a ranger's badge. Cody hesitated for a moment, then slammed open the door to the sheriff's office.

Pete Sloan sat at the big desk. He had a deputy's badge pinned on his stained cowhide vest. When he saw the Ranger he leapt up and tipped over his chair. Before Sloan could recover from his surprise, Cody lunged across the cramped room. Sloan went for the six-gun on his hip, but the Ranger rammed the barrel of Tommy's old rifle into the pit of his stomach. The blow doubled the deputy over, drove the air from his lungs, and left him draped across the desk. Sloan gasped frantically for breath that wouldn't come. Cody thrust the rifle's stock into the base of Sloan's neck and smashed him to the floor.

Havlicek grabbed the outlaw by the collar and dragged the stunned man into a cell. He jerked Sloan's heavy Smith and Wesson .44 from its holster and his knife from its sheath. He shoved them into his own belt and pocketed the spare bullets from Sloan's gunbelt.

"What happened to the sheriff?" Cody demanded, as he leveled Tommy's rifle at the outlaw's chest.

"Havlicek! You're…you're…but you can't be!"

Sloan's eyes were wide with shock and disbelief.

"Yeah, I'm alive," Cody growled. "But you won't be if you don't talk, and right quick."

The Ranger eased back the hammer of the Henry.

"What happened to Mark Carlisle? Don't make me ask you again!"

"Sh… Shot," Sloan stammered, as his eyes rolled in panic.

"Who shot him?"

"I dunno. I mean it, Ranger, I dunno," Sloan whined as Havlicek jabbed the rifle's barrel into his stomach. "Somebody shot him in the back."

"Who had the fool idea to make a lowdown backshooter like you a deputy?" Cody demanded.

"The town council appointed Ned Riley sheriff after Carlisle was shot, and Ned made all of us deputies," Sloan whimpered.

"At Al Kroeger's suggestion?" Cody asked.

"Yeah, at Kroeger's suggestion," Sloan confirmed. "He talked to Silas Dean, the mayor. The two of 'em figured the town needed some tougher lawmen after Carlisle and the liveryman got it."

"Joe Barnes was shot too?" Cody's heart sank.

"Yeah. It looks like he walked in on whoever shot Carlisle. He got drilled too."

"Tommy," Cody whispered.

His heart seemed to leap into his throat. He barely heard Sloan's next words.

"You'll never make it out of this town alive, Ranger," Sloan threatened. "The story goin' round is that you're an outlaw who killed a Ranger and stole his badge. You also killed Deputy Tate and Sheriff Carlisle. Once you're seen, everyone in town'll be gunnin' for you."

"I wouldn't count on it," Cody replied.

The Ranger pulled the bandanna from Sloan's neck, tied a knot in the filthy cloth, and shoved it into the outlaw's mouth. He took Sloan's knife, cut two lengths of rope, and used one to bind Sloan's wrists behind his back.

"I hate to do this," Cody muttered, "but I can't afford to take any chances."

He tapped the Henry's barrel sharply against Sloan's temple and dropped him senseless onto the bunk. Cody tied Sloan's ankles and slammed the cell door shut.

"I've got to get to Tommy before they find him," Cody stated. "I just hope I'm not too late."

14

A hot gust of wind, heavy with the smell of distant rain, slammed into Havlicek as he raced out of the sheriff's office. The Ranger whistled shrilly and dashed recklessly into the street. Yankee whinnied in response, snorted, and tossed his head in protest against the wind-driven sand, as he came from the alley. Cody grabbed Yankee's reins and leaped onto the big paint's back. He pushed him into a hard gallop as soon as he hit the saddle. A cursing teamster was forced to swerve his mules and wagon aside. Reaching the livery stable, Cody slid his horse to a halt. He left the saddle in a rolling dive that ended just inside the doorway. Yankee sought shelter around the corner of the building.

"You happen to be lookin' for this, Ranger?" Earl Dixon growled as Cody rose to one knee.

The Cross R segundo had one arm wrapped around Tommy's neck while he held a pistol to the youngster's head.

"Don't look so surprised," Dixon sneered. "I spotted you goin' into the sheriff's office. Dunno how you're still alive, but that don't matter none, since you won't be for long. Anyhow, I knew Sloan would never be able to handle you by himself. I was headed over there to put a bullet in your back when I saw this here brat sneakin' into town."

Tommy grabbed the pistol of the outlaw. Dixon slammed a fist down on the boy's head, and the kid let go and stopped struggling.

"So, as I was saying, I put two and two together. Somehow

Hanscom's slug didn't finish you, and this lousy kid pulled you out of that canyon. Soon's I saw him, I knew I'd only have to wait right here for you to show up and check on him. Now, do you want to put down that rifle, nice and easy? That gun outta your belt too. Or do I plug the kid?"

"That kid doesn't mean anythin' to me, Dixon," Cody bluffed. "Go right ahead and shoot him. That'll give me the chance to put a slug through your guts."

"Don't try and buffalo me, Havlicek. You're a Texas Ranger, and you sure ain't gonna stand by and watch while I gun down a kid. Besides, this one saved your sorry hide. You're beholden to him. Now, are you gonna drop that gun?"

Cody hesitated for just a moment.

"You've got ten seconds, Ranger," growled Dixon. "Then I blow the kid's brains out."

"Don't do it, Cody," Tommy pleaded. "He's gonna kill you as soon as you put your gun down."

"Just keep your mouth shut, kid," Dixon snapped.

He slapped the barrel of his six-gun against the side of Tommy's head. The boy flinched, his eyes watered from the blow, but he bit his lip against the pain and refused to cry out.

"You'll kill the boy anyway, once you drill me," Cody answered, trying to buy time. "The only way I'll put this gun down is if you give me your word you'll turn him loose."

"Is that all you want, Ranger? Well, why not?"

Dixon laughed harshly.

"Heck, I might even make him a member of our bunch, kind of like a mascot. You'd like that, wouldn't you boy?"

"Never!" Tommy shouted. "I'd rather let you belly-shoot me than turn me into a rotten skunk like you."

"Suit yourself, kid," Dixon retorted. "Time's up, Havlicek. What's it gonna be? You gonna drop that gun, or do I put a bullet in the kid's head?"

"You win, Dixon," Cody conceded.

He started to place Tommy's rifle on the ground. When he did, the boy bit down savagely on Dixon's arm, kicked him in the shin, and pulled free. Tommy ran for the shelter of a stall. Dixon, forgetting about the Ranger in his fury at the boy, swung his gun at Tommy's back. Cody grabbed up the rifle and pulled the trigger. Smoke and flame erupted from the barrel of the old Henry, and Dixon was smashed into a stall partition. The heavy slug slammed into his side. The outlaw's finger tightened on the trigger of his pistol. The bullet passed into the hayloft floor. Dixon's body arched in a spasm and sprawled in the hay and manure littered aisle.

"Tommy, are you all right?" Cody shouted as the boy ran up to him.

"Yeah, Ranger. I'm fine. But they killed Joe," Tommy sobbed.

"I know, son." Cody placed a hand gently on Tommy's head, "and I'm real sorry. That's another thing these renegades have gotta answer for. But those shots are gonna bring everyone in town down on us, so right now we've gotta move fast. Get up in the hayloft and stay there."

"Cody, I still want to help you," Tommy insisted.

"Like I told you before, you already have, when you pulled me out of Blue Canyon," Cody said. "The best way you can help me right now is by keepin' out of the way, so I don't have to be worryin' about you catchin' a stray slug. Just stay out of sight until all this is finished. I'll be back for you. Now get up that ladder."

"All right, Cody," Tommy replied.

He scampered up the loft.

"Lord, if I don't make it outta here, please keep that boy safe," Cody prayed.

He pulled Earl Dixon's gunbelt from the outlaw's body and buckled it around his waist.

"I suppose it's a little too late to ask you to make me right-handed."

He looked at the dead outlaw's pistol hanging on his right hip and sighed.

15

Ned Riley burst into the Dust Devil Saloon while echoes of the shots from the livery stable were still fading away. The other occupants of the saloon turned to gaze questioningly at Alpine's new sheriff. Slade Hanscom calmly looked up from the baize-covered table where he, Monte Harris, and Jorge Randado were engaged in a game of five card stud.

"What the devil is all that shootin' about, Sheriff? And just what are you doin' about it?" Hanscom asked.

"That blasted Ranger's back in town, that's what all the shootin's about," Riley responded. "He knocked out Pete, tied him up and gagged him, and locked him in a cell. I just turned him loose. Pete said Havlicek was headed for the livery stable."

"Havlicek's alive?" Hanscom bellowed. "That's impossible! You saw me plug him. He's lyin' at the bottom of Blue Canyon with one of his own bullets in his guts."

"Mebbe it's impossible," said Riley, "but it wasn't no ghost who got the drop on Pete Sloan. Two women told me they'd seen the Ranger go into the sheriff's office, then leave a few minutes later. Sure enough, when I got Pete woke up, he said Havlicek had come in lookin' for Carlisle. The Ranger must've shot Dixon. I had Dixon watchin' the stable in case any strangers rode into town."

"Earl Dixon can't handle Havlicek by himself," Monte Harris argued. "If he could've, he'd have been over here by now, braggin' how he'd just downed a Texas Ranger."

"Then what're we waitin' for?" Jorge Randado asked as he rose from his chair.

He lifted his Remington, spun the cylinder to check its action, and dropped the pistol loosely back into its holster.

"Let's go get Havlicek," said Randado. "Only this time, I'll make sure he's dead."

"Hold it just a minute," Hanscom ordered, raising his voice for everyone in the Dust Devil to hear.

"I'll personally pay a five hundred dollar bounty to the man who kills that Ranger and brings me his scalp. Sheriff Riley will deputize any man who takes me up on my offer, so everything will be nice and legal. Who's interested?"

A low murmur swept through the smoky saloon as Hanscom's offer was considered. Three players at a card table started to stand up. Miles Thibodeaux, who was sitting with them, looked up from his cards and stared directly into Hanscom's eyes.

"You can take on a Texas Ranger if you want to, Slade, but leave me out of it," the gambler flatly stated. "Yvonne and I came up here from Marathon hopin' to get away from things like this. Isn't that right, darlin'?"

"It certainly is, sugar," Yvonne Waters agreed, as she kissed Thibodeaux lightly on his cheek. "We've both seen enough trouble to last us a lifetime."

"It's bad enough one Ranger's already been killed in these parts, and another's disappeared," Thibodeaux continued. "Even if you should somehow manage to finally kill this one, then what'll happen? You'll have a whole company of Rangers swoopin' down on you. They won't leave until anyone who had a hand in the killing is danglin' from a rope. I don't know about the rest of you, but I'm not hankerin' to wear a hemp necktie."

Thibodeaux resumed dealing cards around the table.

"In or out, boys?"

"Dang it, I've got a hot streak goin'," said one of the players. "Reckon I'll just keep playin'. How about you, Murph?"

"My luck's been pretty good too," his companion agreed.

The player arched one eyebrow and looked thoughtfully at the ceiling. The wind rattled the windows of the saloon and the first few drops of rain splattered on the roof.

"It's fixin' to storm somethin' wicked," said the third player. "I think I'll stay right here where it's nice and dry, play cards, and drink whiskey."

"Yeah," said Murph. "I've got my eye on that pretty brunette. "I guess if I get tired of cards, I'll buy myself a dance or two with her."

As he finished speaking, several other men turned back to the bar and tended their drinks. Mike, the portly bartender, studiously resumed polishing glasses.

"Suit yourself, Miles." Hanscom snarled at the gambler. "I'll remember this later, you can count on it. That goes for the rest of you too."

"If you're still able to remember anything, Slade, once you're through tanglin' with that Ranger," Thibodeaux responded. "Personally, my money's on him."

Deliberately, the gambler turned his attention back to his cards.

"Is every man in here a yella-bellied coward?" Hanscom challenged, running his gaze over the room.

"I wouldn't mind an extra five hundred dollars in my pocket," a towheaded cowboy name Reese replied. "That'd pay for some mighty good times down in Sonora."

His pale blue eyes gleamed in anticipation as he lifted his six-gun from its holster. He slid a bullet into the empty chamber under the hammer, and spun the cylinder.

"How about you, Mack?" Reese asked his partner as he dropped his gun back into the holster.

"I never did care for the Texas Rangers after they arrested my pa and sent him to prison for rustlin'," Mack replied.

"Sorry, honey," Reese told the percentage girl clinging to his arm. "You'll just have to wait awhile longer for that dance. Don't go away. Killing a lone Texas Ranger shouldn't take long."

He kissed her roughly.

"I reckon you can count me in too," said Mack to Hanscom. "My name is Mack Barlow and my pardner here is Reese Campbell."

"We're wastin' time standin' around here jawin'," Ned Riley snapped. "Barlow, Campbell, you're now officially deputized as

Brewster County deputies. Let's get movin'."

*   *   *

Cody looked cautiously up and down the street as he emerged from the livery stable. His eyes watered from the dust and grit being flung into his face by the rising wind. He ran the back of his hand over them to clear his vision and squinted through the haze as he saw Riley and Hanscom. Other men also stepped through the batwings of the Dust Devil. They spread out on the opposite side of the street. Lightning flashed and thunder rumbled in the distance. A few passersby who hadn't already taken shelter from the storm, scrambled for cover. They ducked into stores or ran for their homes.

"Hold it right there!" Cody ordered as he leveled Tommy's ancient rifle at the outlaws. "Texas Ranger! All of you are under arrest, for the murders of Rangers Chance Lowney and Hap Tompkins and other killin's."

"Go to Hades, Ranger!" One of the men yelled through the blowing wind.

"Ranger, you have more lives than a stray cat," Ned Riley shouted back. "I don't know how you managed to climb out of that canyon...but the only way you're leaving here is in a pine box."

As Riley finished speaking the storm broke in all its fury, with wind-driven rain descending in blinding sheets.

"The only dyin' to be done here today will be done by you boys," Cody shouted.

He lifted his voice over the roar of the wind and thunder and continued.

"Unless you throw down your guns and give yourselves up, you'll..."

The Ranger's words were cut short by the sharp crack of a rifle. A bullet tore the Henry from his grasp.

Cody dove onto his stomach and rolled behind a horse trough while Riley and the others went for their guns. He pulled Sloan's Smith and Wesson from his belt to snap a shot at Mack Barlow. Mack had snuck out the back door of the Dust Devil and taken up a position on the roof of the Alpine Mercantile. Barlow dropped his Winchester as Cody's bullet tore into his belly. Barlow seemed to hang on the building's roof for a moment, then tumbled over the edge. The body half buried itself face down in a puddle of mud.

The main street of Alpine erupted in gunfire. Bullets searched out the besieged Ranger. Cody jerked in pain as a slug fired from behind burned along his ribs. He twisted to return fire, and saw Pete Sloan running in terror as Yankee bore down on him. The panicked outlaw screamed in pain when the paint's wicked teeth clamped down on his neck. The horse's shoulder slammed into Sloan's back, knocking him aside like a rag doll.

"Get outta the way, Yank!" Cody shouted. "Before you get shot!"

Yankee galloped behind the barn as his hide steamed from the pouring rain. Cody dove back behind the trough. A bullet whined over his head and another slug drove splinters into his face.

Occupied with Barlow and Sloan, the Ranger did not see Jorge Randado and Monte Harris race across the street. They both gained shelter and positioned themselves to catch the lawman in a deadly crossfire. A bullet from Harris's six-gun bit a chunk of flesh from Cody's upper right arm. It spun him half-around.

"I've got you, Havlicek. There won't be any mistakes this time!" said Randado.

He aimed his pistol at Cody's head and thumbed back the hammer. The outlaw's sneer turned into an expression of shock. Cody fired a bullet into Randado's chest and a second into his forehead. Randado's bullet ricocheted harmlessly and the gunman fell dead.

Cody dove to his left, rolling onto his back. Two bullets from Harris's .44 Colt ripped through the air. Flat on his back, Cody fired twice. His first bullet struck Harris in his left shirt pocket, the second at the V formed by his shirt. The killer was dead before he hit the ground.

The storm continued unabated. Cody punched empty shells from Sloan's revolver. Lightning rent the skies and thunder crashed. The windows rattled in their frames. A gust of wind ripped the sign from the dressmaker's shop and sent it flying down the street. Reese

Campbell rose up from behind the buckboard where he'd taken cover. The sign smacked into the rumps of the wagon's team. The frightened horses reared in total panic. They bolted, broke their reins, and tore off up the road.

Campbell angled across the street to draw a bead on Cody's middle.

"You're mine, Ranger, and so is that five hundred," Campbell called out triumphantly.

Rain poured off the Ranger's body. Sloan's empty gun in hand, he knew he had no chance to get Dixon's gun out. Cody braced himself for hot lead to rip through him. Campbell thumbed back the hammer of his Colt and aimed at the lawman. Two shots rang out. The gunman screamed as he clawed at his stomach. A red stain spread across his shirt. The light faded from Campbell's pale eyes as he collapsed.

"Just thought we'd even up the odds a little," a familiar voice called.

Cody glanced across the street to see Jed and Deke, the cowboys he'd picked the bar fight with when he first rode into Alpine. They grinned at him, their smoking six-guns still in hand. Cody waved in gratitude while he shoved the last of Sloan's bullets into the Smith and Wesson.

"Behind you, Ranger!" Deke shouted a warning.

Ned Riley burst through the doors of the Alpine Dry Goods Emporium. Cody whirled and fired at the same moment as Riley. Riley buckled to his knees, and two more shots sounded from the Ranger's pistol. Riley lay on his back, eyes staring unblinkingly at the vivid bolts of lightning. The rain washed away the blood pooling around his body.

"Hanscom!" Cody's voice cut through the maelstrom. "You're on your own now. I'm comin' after you!"

Deliberately, the Ranger came to his feet and tossed aside Sloan's empty pistol. Slade Hanscom stood on the boardwalk in front of the Dust Devil, where he was protected from the storm by the wooden awning. Once again Cody had to run the back of his hand across his mud-spattered face and eyes to clear his vision. He started toward the embittered former government clerk.

"You're gonna hang, Slade Hanscom!" the Ranger shouted. "Bet a hat on that, unless you've got the guts to go for your gun…or should I say my gun."

Cody corrected himself as he saw his own Colt Peacemaker in the holster at Hanscom's hip.

"C'mon, Slade," Cody urged and walked steadily forward, closing the distance between them. "You can beat me real easy. What're you waitin' for, Hanscom? I thought you wanted to put a couple of slugs through my guts. Well, now's your chance."

Hanscom stood frozen in place. He grew deathly pale while the Ranger closed the gap to less than twenty feet. Dixon's six-gun still hung at Cody's right hip.

"What's the matter?" he taunted Hanscom. "You sure weren't afraid to throw a slug into me before when Riley and his men stood behind you and I had no gun."

The distance between the two men had narrowed to less than ten feet.

"I knew you didn't have the guts to face a man head on, Slade!" Cody snarled.

Hanscom hesitated, his hand quivering as it hovered over his gun. Then, his nerve broke under the angry glare of Cody's icy blue eyes. Hanscom raised his hands over his head.

"You're right, Havlicek. I don't have the guts."

A rifle shot rang out and dropped Cody to one knee. A bullet ripped through his thigh. When the Ranger fell, Hanscom jerked the Peacemaker from his holster and pulled the trigger.

Hanscom's hastily fired shot missed. Cody made sure he didn't get a second chance. The ranger drew the pistol from Dixon's right holster, and fired twice. Both bullets tore into Hanscom's belly. Hanscom tumbled off the boardwalk into the muddy street. Someone fired another rifle slug and it pierced the air over the Ranger's head. Cody shifted to his right and sent three bullets into the doorway of the Alpine Advisor. Al Kroeger threw up his hands and dropped a rifle. He stumbled out of his office with three Ranger bullets in his chest. The newspaperman fell backwards, crashed through the window of his office, and landed face-up amidst shards of shattered glass.

Cody pushed himself painfully to his feet, his shoulders slumped in exhaustion. After a brief glance at the men sprawled in the mud, he turned to where Slade Hanscom lay on his back. The dying man tried to lift Havlicek's stolen Peacemaker. Cody wrenched the gun from Hanscom's fingers and shoved it into his own belt.

"Blast it. I thought sure…we had you beat…Havlicek," Hanscom gasped.

A thin froth of blood formed on his lips. The slackening rain turned the puddle beneath him pink.

"Get me the doc," Hanscom pleaded as he shivered with cold.

"Doctor Trombley's already on his way," one of the bystanders stated.

Cody looked around in revulsion as a wave of nausea churned his stomach. It never failed to amaze and disgust him how swiftly the morbidly curious gathered. Not one of these people had raised so much as a finger to help him. Deep inside, Cody realized that most of them wouldn't have cared if it had been him lying there as long as the blood lust was satisfied.

Slade Hanscom's quavering voice snapped Havlicek out of his dreary reverie.

"Dunno how you…got out of…Blue Canyon," Hanscom muttered. "The buzzards should be… tearin' on your bones."

"Never mind that, Hanscom," Cody responded. "You haven't got much time. You might want to come clean before you face your Maker."

"Yeah," Hanscom weakly replied, "Guess it doesn't matter…if I admit it, now that…Kroeger's done for. He wasn't…the real boss."

Hanscom tried to laugh, instead choked on blood welling in his throat.

"I'm not gonna tell you, and you'll…never figure out who…the real boss is, Havlicek. Not in a hundred years."

Hanscom shuddered one final time as his body went limp and his eyes closed.

"It doesn't matter if you tell me or not," Cody said to the dead man. "I already know."

The Ranger turned away from Hanscom's body. He limped heavily through the ankle deep muck. His rain soaked clothes clung to his frame. His boot was filling with blood running from the bullet hole in his thigh. He climbed the steps to the boardwalk and wearily went into the Alpine Mercantile. Silas Dean stood behind a counter cluttered with merchandise. His gray eyes were masked by thick spectacles.

"Don't kill me, please, Ranger…or should I say Jim Smith, the gunman," Dean pleaded.

"Stop that!" said the Ranger.

"Please don't gun me down—like you did the real Ranger whose badge you stole."

"I told you to stop that nonsense!" Cody said again.

"You'll kill me! Like you shot Deputy Tate, Sheriff Carlisle, and Joe Barnes."

"The name's Cody Havlicek of the Texas Rangers, as you well know," Cody stated, his blue eyes dark with anger. "And I have no intention of killin' you. I am placin' you under arrest, Silas Dean, for conspiracy to commit several murders, includin' those of two Texas Rangers."

"You can't arrest an innocent man!" declared Dean.

"I can and I will! You're being arrested for conspiracy to commit arson of Anders' photography shop, for attempted murder of myself, and I'm positive a large list of other charges."

"I had nothing to do with those killings, or any other crime!" Dean protested. "Those were all the doings of a vicious gang of outlaws."

"You sure did," Cody growled. "That vicious gang of outlaws was workin' for you, Dean. You were in cahoots with Al Kroeger. The two of you planned on takin' over this whole section of Texas."

"You can't possibly prove any of those ridiculous charges, Ranger," Dean challenged.

"Oh, yes, I can," Cody disagreed. "For starters, you let one of those men in here so he could try and nail me from your roof. That's enough evidence right there to hold you on suspicion. Second,"

Cody bluffed, "Slade Hanscom lived long enough to talk."

"But you won't live long enough to prove anything," Dean said.

He reached inside his apron to pull out a Derringer.

Cody lunged across the counter. His hand shot out and grabbed the mercantile owner's wrist. Cody bent his wrist back and bones cracked. Dean let loose with a high-pitched shout. The Derringer went off; its bullet shattered the store front window.

"You just gave me all the proof I need," Cody stated. "Start headin' for the jail, Mayor."

He shoved Dean out the door and onto the stairs as a last rumble of thunder from the receding storm echoed down the street.

"Cody! Cody! You're all right!"

Tommy rushed up to him and Yankee followed.

"I saw the whole thing from the hayloft," Tommy exclaimed breathlessly. "I was afraid they'd get you. I'm sure glad they didn't."

"I thought I told you to stay put until I came for you," Cody growled in feigned anger, "and that meant both of you."

Yank rubbed at the Ranger's pocket.

"Forget it, Yank. I've had a few other things to do besides buyin' you candy. And, as for you, Tommy Mashburn…"

"I'm sorry, Cody, but I just had to know for sure what happened to you."

He stopped to stare at the bloody bullet hole in Havlicek's leg.

"Hadn't you better get to the doc's and get patched up?"

"I'm doin' okay for now," Cody answered, "and I guess it's all right your comin' to check on me. I've still got to finish things up here. Keep an eye on Yank for me."

"Sure," Tommy agreed.

Deke and Jed, Cody's two adversaries from the Dust Devil, walked up.

"There anythin' we can do to help out, Ranger?" Deke asked.

"Yeah," Cody replied. "Thanks for savin' my hide. That kid had me dead to rights. I figured he was gonna punch my ticket to Boot Hill. I'm in need of a couple of deputies. I'd like to hand you two the job."

He nodded at the Alpine Mercantile's owner.

"Silas Dean is under arrest for murder. Think you can haul him over to the jail for me?"

"We sure can, Ranger," Jed answered. "Sorry we didn't take a hand sooner, but we weren't positive about you. The story was you'd gone bad. But, when we saw those hombres gangin' up and tryin' to backshoot you..."

"Besides," Deke continued, grinning, "you pack a mean wallop. We couldn't let a man who can hit like that get himself all shot up."

"*Por nada*," Cody replied, grinning in return.

"This jasper's still alive, Ranger, but your cayuse sure did a number on him," Mike, the Dust Devil's bartender called out.

The barkeep stood with his sawed-off shotgun aimed at Pete Sloan's chest. Sloan was propped against the livery stable's wall, groaning as he clutched his torn, bloodied neck and shoulder.

"Sloan's lucky that Yank didn't kill him," Cody replied. "He's done for more than a few renegades."

"What do you want me to do with him?" Mike questioned.

"He's under arrest on the same charges as Dean," Cody answered. "Deke, take care of him for me."

"It'll be a pure pleasure, Ranger," Deke grinned. "I'll take both to the doc and get them patched up, then we'll lock these hombres away."

"I appreciate that," Cody said.

He turned to the boy.

"Tommy?"

"Yeah, Cody?" the boy eagerly responded.

"Now it's time to get me to the doc's."

The worn-out Ranger took one faltering step and pitched on his face in the muck.

16

Cody awakened in an unfamiliar, dimly lit room to the mingled scents of soaps, medicines, and clean sheets. There was the pressure of bandages around his arm, leg, and ribs. He looked around the room and spotted Tommy curled up in a chair next to his bed, sound asleep. The boy held Cody's badge clutched tightly in his hand.

The door opened and a white-haired elderly man entered. Cody put a cautioning finger to his lips and nodded toward Tommy.

"You needn't worry," came the whispered response. "That boy wouldn't leave your side, no matter how hard I tried to persuade him. He's completely exhausted. We won't wake him. I'm Doctor Horace Trombley. I must say, I'm certainly surprised and glad to see you come around so quickly. I understand you're Texas Ranger Cody Havlicek."

"That's right, Doc," Cody smiled in answer.

"Well, unfortunately, you've taken quite a beating, Ranger Havlicek." Trombley pulled back the sheets that were covering Cody. "I need to recheck your bandages."

"Doc, most folks just call me Cody."

"Then Cody it shall be," Trombley agreed.

The physician checked Cody's bandages, clucking to himself and shaking his head several times as he worked.

"I'll need to redress the wound in your leg and change the bandage," he explained. "The bullet didn't lodge in your thigh, but I need to make sure the wound drains properly and doesn't become infected."

He opened a cabinet and removed a brown glass bottle.

"This will sting somewhat."

"Doc, after what I've been through the last few days, I think I can handle just about anythin' you might dish out."

"Very well," Trombley responded.

He commenced to unwrap the blood-stained bandage.

"This really doesn't look bad at all," the doctor noted.

He washed the holes in Cody's thigh and dried them.

"Here comes the part that will smart," the physician warned.

He opened the bottle and poured a carbolic solution into the bullet holes. Cody winced against the burning pain, gritting his teeth so as not to cry out and awaken Tommy.

"Well, Cody," Trombley finally announced as he rebandaged the Ranger's thigh. "Your wounds aren't really all that serious. The one in your side, while messy and no doubt painful, is little more than a scratch. That bullet didn't even nick a rib. The wound in the right arm merely cut out a piece of flesh. While you won't be able to use your gun arm well, you won't even need a sling. The hole in your leg is the most serious. Even that bullet went through cleanly. None of the slugs struck any bones, but you did lose a considerable amount of blood."

"Doc, I'm left-handed, so that bullet hole in my arm won't affect my shootin' one bit," Cody explained.

"I didn't realize that," Trombley replied. "I just naturally assumed you were right handed. After all, you were wearing your holster on your right hip when you were brought in."

"That wasn't my holster. I sorta borrowed it. I'll be up and around in a couple of hours?" Cody eagerly asked.

"Not quite so fast, Ranger," Trombley responded. "Let me clarify. I meant your bullet wounds aren't all that serious. However, you have a very severe case of sun poisoning and a significant fever. This, along with some pretty deep bruises. You're also suffering from dehydration and several infected cuts. I'm rather amazed your kidneys are still functioning. Mostly you're just plain worn out. You won't be leaving here for a few days, at the very least."

"Doc, I can't stay in bed," Cody protested. "That's impossible.

I've got prisoners to look after and a lot of loose ends to tie up. I also need to get telegrams off to Cap'n Blawcyzk at Ranger Headquarters and to my wife. And I've gotta check on my horse."

"Ranger, perhaps my explanation of your condition wasn't clear enough," Trombley answered. "I can't give you permission to get out of that bed. You are still in danger of developing blood poisoning. Whether you like it or not, you'll be confined to bed for at least five days."

"I've really gotta get outta here, Doc," Cody insisted. "By the way, I'm also starvin'. I haven't had anythin' to eat for the past several days but a few strips of jerky and a couple of hardtack biscuits."

Trombley rubbed his salt and pepper beard thoughtfully, seeing the determination in Havlicek's eyes.

"Well, I can't let you out of bed, but at least the fact that you're hungry is a good sign. You can have some beef or chicken broth along with weak coffee or tea, but that's all."

"I was thinkin' more along the lines of a thick, juicy steak," Cody retorted. "Now give me my clothes so I can get the heck outta here."

"You don't really have any clothes," Trombley chuckled. "There wasn't much left of them when you were brought in. But, since you're so determined, I'll offer you a compromise. I understand you've appointed a couple of men to act as deputies until Sheriff Carlisle is up and about again."

"Hold on a minute," Cody exclaimed, surprise evident in his voice. "Mark Carlisle? I thought he'd been killed, shot in the back."

"I just assumed you knew about the sheriff. Carlisle was shot in the back. Fortunately for him, the bullet missed his spine. I was able to dig that slug out of him, and he should make a full recovery. I expect him to come around in the next day or so. He's in the next room right now, along with Joe from the livery stable."

"Joe Barnes!" Cody incredulously exclaimed. "Doc, either I've missed somethin' here, or I'm in far worse shape than I thought. I was told Barnes was killed by the same person who shot Sheriff Carlisle."

"I don't know who gave you that information, but they were misinformed. Joe Barnes was shot in the chest at close range. I was able to remove the bullet without any complications. You'll probably be able to speak with him sometime tomorrow. By the way, I recommend you take some laudanum to help you sleep."

"Uh-uh, Doc," Cody disagreed. "That stuff dulls my senses too much. I'll pass."

"All right. If you should become too uncomfortable, please don't hesitate to ask."

"Doc, does Tommy know about Joe and Mark?" Cody asked.

"Yes, he does. He was quite pleased to discover both men are still alive. However, he seemed most concerned about you. He helped carry you in here and he never once left your side, even while I was treating you. Tommy seems like quite a brave young man."

"He's a smart lad," Cody remarked and smiled. "He saved my life when he pulled me out of Blue Canyon."

Cody paused to take a deep breath.

"But Doc, I still haven't seen you go for clothes," he protested.

"My, but you Texas Rangers are thick-headed, aren't you? I can't allow you to leave until you've regained some of your strength. I would be willing to send for one of those men you've appointed as deputies. I'm certain they will be able to assist you."

"All right, Doc—seein' as you're givin' me no choice."

"That's right. I'm not," Trombley retorted.

"Then I'll go along with your orders for now."

A broad smile crossed the Ranger's face as his blue eyes twinkled devilishly.

"I'll go along about the deputy. But I'm sure not givin' in about my grub. I want the biggest steak you can come up with, and a thick brew of black coffee. Unless, you'd care to head on over to the Dust Devil and get a nice cold bottle or two of sarsaparilla for me."

"I suppose a good meal wouldn't hurt." Trombley conceded. "It would certainly help build up your blood. My wife is out of town, visiting friends in Baton Rouge, but Marta, our housekeeper, will be preparing supper shortly. I'll send her for one of the deputies, then have her fix you something as soon as she returns."

"That's fine," Cody agreed. "What time is it, anyway?"

Trombley pulled a big silver turnip watch from his vest pocket.

"It's just about four o'clock in the afternoon."

"You mean I've only been out a couple of hours?" Cody asked.

"Not exactly," the physician explained. "It's four o'clock in the afternoon, two days after the gunfight. Ranger, you've been unconscious for more than forty-eight hours."

"Then I really do need to get some things done," Cody replied. "Can I ask Marta for another favor?"

"Certainly," Trombley agreed.

"On her way to find Jed or Deke, would you please have her stop by the county clerk's office and tell him to come see me? There's some more records I need to examine, and I can sure do that while I'm lyin' around in bed. I want to talk with the clerk before he goes home for the night."

"That shouldn't be a problem," Trombley answered. "Now why don't you try and get some more rest? I'll wake you when the clerk or your deputy arrives."

"I've already slept the clock twice around, Doc," Cody grinned.

"I know, but more sleep will still do you a world of good," Trombley explained.

"I reckon I could stand a little more shut-eye," Cody admitted, yawning. "Make sure you wake me up the minute Jed, Deke, or the clerk gets here."

"You have my word," Trombley assured the Ranger as he stepped out of the room and closed the door.

Cody lay staring at the ceiling, absorbed in thought. Had it really only been three days ago that Tommy had pulled him out of Blue Canyon? Three days since the desperate gunbattle in the streets of Alpine? To his weary mind, it seemed as if months had passed since he'd ridden out of Austin, not just a few weeks.

"Well, at least you'll be headin' home in only a few days, Ranger," he quietly assured himself.

Tommy stirred in his chair next to Havlicek's bed and glanced over at the Ranger.

"Cody?" he whispered. "Are you awake?"

"I sure am," the Ranger replied. "Sorry if I woke you, Tommy."

"You didn't. How're you feelin'?"

Cody managed to chuckle.

"Not all that bad for an hombre who's been shot. Tommy, I understand you helped drag my carcass down here to the doc's. You stayed with me ever since. Thanks, son, for that, and a whole lot more."

"I couldn't let my pardner down, could I? We are still pards, aren't we, Cody?" Tommy asked as his eyes grew moist.

"We sure are," Cody replied. "You can bet a hat on that."

"I've got your badge here for you, Ranger."

Tommy held out his right hand with Havlicek's Ranger silver star on silver circle flat in his palm.

"You hold onto that for now," Cody ordered, then chuckled as he glanced at his bare chest. "Besides, I don't exactly have any place to pin it on me right now. You keep that badge safe for me. I'm also gonna depend on you to take care of Yankee until I'm up and around again. Seein' as you and him are gettin' along all right. Will you do that for me?"

"You can count on me," Tommy assured him.

"Good. Then I'm gonna get some more shut-eye. Jed or Deke are supposed to be on their way. Wake me as soon as one of 'em shows up."

Cody turned onto his side and pulled the covers up to his chin.

"Sure, Cody," Tommy agreed.

The Ranger's eyes closed, his breathing settled into the deep, regular rhythm of a man sleeping peacefully.

17

Havlicek was awakened by a tapping on his door.

"Ranger?" a soft feminine voice, with just the hint of a Spanish accent, inquired. "Are you awake?"

"Yes," Cody sleepily mumbled.

"Deputy Deke has arrived. Are you ready to see him?"

"Sure. Send him right on in."

At Cody's affirmative response, Deke poked his head through the doorway. The newly appointed deputy grinned as he stepped into the room.

"Howdy, boss. Great to see you're awake and doin' all right."

Deke nodded at Tommy, who was still keeping vigil over his wounded friend.

"I see you're still here, Tommy. Sure hope you got some rest," Deke smiled.

"You'd best forget that 'boss' stuff, if you want to keep your job, deputy," Havlicek said with a grin. "Just call me Cody. Y'know, I never did get either yours or Jed's last names."

"Mine is Morris," Deke answered, "and Jed's is Hanes. He'll be along in a bit."

"Who's keepin' an eye on the prisoners?" Cody questioned.

"Wes Adams, our boss from the Circle M," Deke explained. "When we didn't get back to the ranch with his supplies, he came looking. Marta stopped by the jail and said you needed to see us. She also spoke with Roy Dobbins, the county clerk who refused your request. So we pressed Wes into service as a jail guard while

Jed went to persuade Dobbins it would be in his best interest to visit you."

"Everythin' quiet otherwise?"

"Quiet as a church on Monday mornin'. Silas Dean won't say a word to anyone. The doc patched up Pete Sloan and Dean's wrist. Sloan was still sleepin' when I left. And I nearly forgot. He asked me to pass you word he wants to make a deal, and that he's willin' to spill his guts to save his worthless hide."

"Any deal'll be up to the court, not me," Cody responded.

Marta quietly entered the room, carrying a tray.

"Ranger Havlicek, I have your supper here," she announced.

"Bring it on in."

Cody grinned in anticipation as Marta, a dark haired woman in her early fifties, came into the room. She placed a tray containing a huge steak, potatoes, pinto beans, and apple pie next to his bed. There was also a steaming pot of black coffee.

"Doctor Trombley says you're not to overeat," Marta warned.

The housekeeper turned her attention to Tommy.

"I have your supper waiting in the kitchen, Tommy. Maybe you're hungry?"

"Am I ever!"

"Go ahead, kid," Cody laughed. "I'll see you later."

Tommy dashed from the room.

*　　*　　*

When Havlicek was halfway through his supper, Jed Hanes arrived.

"Howdy, Cody," he called out.

Jed pushed a man who appeared to be in his forties into the room ahead of him.

"This here hombre is Roy Dobbins, the Brewster County clerk. Dobbins, I shouldn't have to tell you this is Texas Ranger Cody Havlicek."

The county clerk mopped his sweaty brow with a clean white handkerchief as he stared nervously at the Ranger.

"Thanks for talkin' Mr. Dobbins into payin' me a visit, Jed," Cody replied.

The Ranger's eyes glittered as he turned his gaze on the visibly shaking clerk.

"I appreciate you coming, Mr. Dobbins. I would have come to your office myself and saved you the trouble, but the doc won't let me out of here for a couple of days."

"This is really quite irregular," Dobbins sniffed. "I certainly hope you don't intend to cause me any difficulties."

"Not at all, unless you refuse to cooperate," Cody coolly replied. "I just need to see copies of the transactions and deed transfers for the sale of Peter Hunt's ranch, as well as those for Ross Moore's harness shop, Paolo Alvarado's freight line, and Ted Boscobel's feed store."

As Dobbins began to sputter a protest, Havlicek's voice hardened.

"Mr. Dobbins, those documents are all a matter of public record. I don't need a warrant to see them. Don't force me to get a court order to obtain those files. If that becomes necessary I'll charge you with obstruction of justice, conspiracy to defraud, and accessory to murder. It also wouldn't surprise me if I dug deep enough to find you've been accepting bribes. Do I make myself clear, sir?"

"Perfectly clear, Ranger," Dobbins grumbled. "I'll have those papers for you the first thing in the morning."

"You'll give those documents to Deputy Hanes tonight," Cody ordered. "I don't want them to mysteriously disappear, or perhaps be destroyed by an 'accidental' fire. There's already been one arson committed, and I'm not takin' any chances on another. Jed, go with him, right now."

"My office is closed for the night," Dobbins protested.

"I assume you have the key," Cody retorted.

"If he doesn't, I do," Jed answered, grinning.

He lifted his six-gun from its holster.

"This'll open any lock. Let's go, Dobbins."

Jed grabbed the clerk by his shoulder, spun him around, and marched him out the door.

Deke, who had watched the exchange between the Ranger and

the county clerk in bemused silence, broke into laughter.

"I think you convinced friend Dobbins to cooperate, Cody."

"Let's hope so," Havlicek replied. "Those records are the evidence I need to keep Silas Dean behind bars for good, or perhaps hang him. Deke, I need you to do me a couple more favors."

"Just ask."

"First off, I never have had the chance to apologize to you and Jed for startin' that fight with you boys in the Dust Devil."

"Heck, Cody, is that all that's botherin' you? If us Circle M hands don't get into a good barroom brawl at least once a month, we figure we're gettin' soft. Would've been a mite easier on you if you'd let us know beforehand you were a Ranger, though."

"I didn't have time," Cody explained. "Besides, if you'd known who I was, things wouldn't have been so convincin'. That fight had to look real."

"Those punches you hit us with sure were real enough," Deke grinned. "What were those other favors you wanted?"

"I need you to send two wires for me. The first one is to Captain Blawcyzk at Ranger Headquarters."

Cody took a paper and pencil from the bedstand and composed a brief message. *Job finished. Men dead or in custody who are responsible for murders of Rangers Lowney and Tompkins and others . CH.*

"That it?" Deke asked, as Cody passed the lined yellow sheet to him.

"Nope." Cody smiled as he wrote out another message. "This is the more important of the two."

He passed the paper to Deke, who read, *Sarah Havlicek, CH Bar Ranch, Buda, Texas. Am safe and will return home soon as possible. Give my love to Andy and Abby. Miss you all. Love, Cody.*

"That goes to my wife and kids," the Ranger explained.

"I'll make sure they both go right out," Deke promised. "Is there anythin' else?"

"Yeah, there is. The other favor I need is more difficult."

"What is it?" Deke asked.

"I'd like you to round up a couple of men who'd be willin' to ride out to Blue Canyon. Tommy will show you exactly where to go. Ranger Hap Tompkins' remains are on a rock bench about thirty feet down from the canyon's rim. I'd sure appreciate it if you could bring Hap back here for a decent burial."

"That wouldn't be a favor, Ranger," Deke answered. "It would be an honor. We'll start out first thing in the mornin'."

"Thanks, Deke," Cody replied. "You'd better get on back to the jail before your boss starts wonderin' where you disappeared to. On your way out ask Doc Trombley to come see me for a minute."

"Somethin' wrong, Cody? You feelin' a mite sick?"

"Nope, it's nothin' like that. I just want to ask the doc about the slugs he dug out of Mark Carlisle and Joe Barnes. With any luck at all, by the day after tomorrow I'll have everythin' just about cleared up. Hey, I nearly forgot. I do need one last favor."

"Yes, Ranger?"

"See if you or Jed can find my gunbelt. Slade Hanscom was carryin' my six-gun, so I figure my belt's stashed at his place or the sheriff's office. Left-handed gunbelts aren't all that easy to come by. My Winchester is probably with it too."

"I can do that," Deke said.

"Also, I kinda need a Stetson, and a new set of duds. I don't know where you'll come up with 'em, since Dean's in jail and the mercantile's padlocked. I've got the money you'll need in my jeans pocket."

"From what I hear tell, the town council's already appointed a receiver to run the mercantile until Dean comes to trial," Deke explained. "The town can't afford to have it closed for very long. It's the only store for thirty miles in any direction. I'll get you some new duds. Is that it, Cody?"

"That's all I can think of for now."

"Then I'll say good night. Be back first thing in the mornin'."

Once the deputy left, Cody spent the next several minutes thanking the Lord for rescuing him from the depths of Blue Canyon. He fell asleep with a prayer on his lips.

18

As reluctant as he was to admit it, Havlicek was far too weak to get out of bed the next day. Tommy and the two deputies, along with several other men departed at sunrise for Blue Canyon. The Ranger was left alone with his breakfast. After eating, Cody carefully studied the documents Jed Hanes had brought from the county clerk's office. As he'd expected, they confirmed his theory about Silas Dean's and Al Kroeger's plans. He composed a second telegram to Captain Blawcyzk that Marta delivered to the Western Union office for him. With those chores done, Cody dozed the rest of the morning and awakened shortly before Jed, Deke, and Tommy returned.

"Did you recover Hap Tompkins remains?" he asked as soon as they walked through the door.

"We sure did, Cody," Jed answered. "It took a mite of doin', but his bones are at the undertaker's. We figure on holdin' off on the funeral until you can be there. Since no one here ever met Tompkins, the townsfolk felt it'd be best for you to say a few words."

"That'll be just fine. Thanks to all of you, especially Tommy."

"It wasn't any trouble."

"How's Yank doin'?"

"Just fine. He really misses you, though," Tommy said.

"That ornery cayuse like to tore my head off when I walked by him," Deke complained.

"That's ol' Yank all right," Cody chuckled. "Sorry, Deke. I didn't get the chance to warn you about him."

"Well, you don't have to now," Deke laughed as Doctor Trombley entered the room. "I won't go anywhere near him again."

"I hate to break this up," the physician apologized. "But Ranger Havlicek's bandages have to be changed. Tommy, Marta has some fresh-baked sugar cookies for you in the kitchen."

"I'll be right back."

He dashed out of the room.

"*Adios* for now, Cody," Deke said. "Jed'n I'll stop by later."

*   *   *

"Your fever has broken, and your wounds show no sign of infection," Doctor Trombley said. "I've removed those old stitches and I can see that slash across your abdomen has healed nicely. Doctor Tarbell did a good job sewing you up."

Marta brought in the Ranger's supper.

"You should be able to get out of bed and walk around your room in a day or so."

"Doc, I'm leavin' this room tomorrow," Cody insisted. "It's not doin' me a doggone bit of good just lyin' here in bed."

"We'll discuss that in the morning," the physician replied. "Eat your supper. I concede, the big dinner last night didn't hurt you."

"See, Doc, I was right about that, and I'm right about gettin' out of this dadblasted bed."

"Good night, Ranger," the doctor said. "I'll talk with you in the morning."

An hour later Cody was lying on his back, half-asleep, when someone knocked on the door.

"Evenin', Ranger. Up for some company?"

Miles Thibodeaux entered Havlicek's room, riffling a deck of cards in his hand.

"I thought perhaps a few hands of poker would help you pass the time."

"They sure would, Miles."

Cody grinned as he shoved himself to a seated position, propping himself against his pillows.

Yvonne Waters, clad in an emerald dress, came into the room.

"Yipes!" Cody yelled.

He grabbed for the sheets, pulling them up to cover his abdomen. She gazed with frank admiration at the Ranger's broad chest.

"You didn't warn me you had a lady with you, Miles. I'm not decent." Cody complained.

"You don't need to be shy, Ranger," Yvonne laughed. "You sure look pretty decent to me. What I've brought you will make up for any embarrassment."

She uncovered a wicker basket and produced four bottles of sarsaparilla.

"Yvonne, you're an angel!" Cody exclaimed. "Thank you."

"I know," Yvonne sweetly replied. "And you're welcome."

She kissed Cody lightly on his cheek and the Ranger flushed.

"Ranger, are you goin' to play cards, or flirt with my woman all night?" Thibodeaux questioned.

"I was gonna play poker," Cody grinned, "but I'm beginnin' to think you brought her along to distract me."

"Cody, that thought never entered my head for a minute." Thibodeaux laughed. "I take it you're no longer interested in a game."

"Start shufflin' those cards," Cody ordered. "I'm gonna beat the pants offa you, gamblin' man."

"Well, you've already lost your shirt, Ranger," Yvonne laughed. "Let's hope you have better luck with the cards."

For the next two hours, Cody and Thibodeaux played poker while Yvonne stood alongside the gambler. Cody was several dollars down when he stretched wearily.

"Just a couple more hands, Miles, then I'm gonna have to call it a night. I'm gettin' kinda tired," he yawned.

"Whatever you wish," Thibodeaux shrugged.

He shuffled the cards and turned over an eight of diamonds.

"Cody, you look uncomfortable," Yvonne noted. "Let me fluff up your pillows for you."

"You don't have to do that," Cody protested. "I'm fine."

She left Thibodeaux to stand alongside Cody's bed and lean over the Ranger. Yvonne partially blocked Havlicek's view of the gambler. Thibodeaux's hand slid under his coat to draw a pistol from his shoulder holster. He never got the chance to fire his gun. Cody reached under his blankets and pulled the trigger of his hidden Colt. Thibodeaux was slammed against the wall as the .45 slug plowed into his chest. The Ranger moved back on the bed while Thibodeaux sagged to the floor. Yvonne cursed, pulled a knife from her garter, and slashed at the lawman. The blade cut through his blankets but missed his ribs. Cody grabbed and twisted the knife from the woman's wrist.

"Take it easy, lady!"

Yvonne reached again for the knife, and the Ranger turned his Colt to aim it at her chest.

"I've never shot a woman, but if you try for that knife again, I might have to. I've been expectin' this. You'd better stand quiet."

Doctor Trombley burst into the room. His gaze settled on the bullet hole in Cody's blanket, which still smoldered. His eyes shifted to Miles Thibodeaux, who lay slumped against the wall.

"Cody, what the devil's going on in here?" he demanded.

"Got another patient for you, Doc," Cody replied.

The physician knelt alongside the gambler.

"You mean a body for the undertaker," Trombley corrected. "You shot too well, Ranger. He's dead."

"He forced it," Cody answered.

Yvonne cursed him bitterly, then began to weep.

"I didn't have any choice. He was too fast."

"I'll get one of the deputies for you," Trombley said.

"No need, Doc," Jed Hanes announced.

He came into the room with a shotgun at the ready.

"Cody, what in blazes happened?" Hanes asked.

"The gambler and woman tried to kill me. Yvonne Waters is under arrest. Lock her up."

19

The next morning, over Doctor Trombley's objections, Cody was up and out of his sickbed. Deke Morris brought new clothes and a Stetson. After bathing and shaving, the Ranger hurriedly dressed. He tugged on his jeans and shrugged into the new light blue shirt.

"They fit pretty good," Cody noted. "Appreciate you gettin' them for me."

He crimped the brim of the cream colored Stetson and adjusted the hat on his blonde hair.

"I guess that old sayin' about clothes makin' the man is true. They can even make an ugly hombre like you look good," chuckled Deke.

He handed Havlicek his Winchester and gunbelt.

"Found it in Slade Hanscom's room at the hotel."

The Ranger checked the loads in his pistol, holstered it, then buckled the belt around his waist. He took comfort in the familiar weight. Cody slid into his vest and knotted a clean bandanna around his neck.

"Let's go, Deke."

Cody stepped into the sunshine, the early morning rays glittered brilliantly off the badge pinned to his vest. He and Deke crossed the street and walked into the sheriff's office.

"Howdy, Cody. You're lookin' pretty good, considerin'," Jed greeted the Ranger. "How are you feelin'?"

"Just fine, now that I'm outta bed. How's the prisoners?"

"They won't talk to anyone, not even each other, if that's what you're gettin' at," Jed answered. "You gonna question 'em?"

"Not right now," Cody decided. "Let 'em sit and stew awhile. I'd rather wait until I get my telegram from Headquarters anyway."

"Any chance you'll tell us what's goin' on?" Deke asked.

"Nope," Cody replied. "Just make sure you guard the three prisoners. I've got a few stops to make. I'll see both of you later."

"Where you headed?" Deke asked.

"To the livery stable," Cody grinned in reply.

"I should've known," Deke groaned. "Get outta here. We'll check in with you later."

"Sure," Cody agreed. "By then I might be able to tell you more."

At the livery stable, Tommy had temporarily taken charge. Yankee pawed frantically at the door of his stall. He whickered a noisy greeting to Cody when he entered the barn. The big horse buried his muzzle in the Ranger's middle. Cody grunted at the paint's exuberant greeting. He scratched behind the gelding's ears and stroked his neck. Yankee dropped his nose to the Ranger's hip pocket to beg for his expected treat.

"Sure, you don't care that I was nearly shot to pieces, as long as I'm here to hand over your peppermints," Cody scolded.

He dug in his jeans and produced a candy stick.

While Yankee crunched down on the sweet, Cody examined the bullet wound on his horse's flank. He noted the scar was rapidly fading, and that the paint's shining chestnut and white coat was newly brushed.

Tommy came through the back door of the barn and rolled an empty wheelbarrow up to Yankee's stall.

"Cody! I didn't expect you quite yet," Tommy exclaimed. "Does Yank look all right to you?"

"He looks just great," Cody assured the boy. "You've been doin' a fine job with him. I'm sure thankful. Brownie looks good too."

Tommy's mare was stretching her neck over the partition of her stall to nuzzle Yankee's shoulder.

"For that matter, the whole barn looks great. Joe'll be real pleased to see what you've done for him," Cody praised.

"Thanks," Tommy answered, as he shoveled soiled bedding out of Yankee's stall. "I sure hope Joe gives me a job permanent-like, once he's feelin' better."

"As soon as he sees how you've cared for this place, I'm certain he'll give you a job. Listen, I've got a few more stops to make. I'll see you tonight. Yank, you behave yourself."

A final pat to his gelding and Cody left the stable and crossed the street to the Western Union office. He sent another long message to Austin. Still weak from his ordeal of the past few days, he returned to his room at Doctor Trombley's. Before taking a nap, he spoke with Joe Barnes. The hostler was still heavily sedated, and not quite sure of his surroundings. Later in the morning, Doctor Trombley redressed Cody's wounds. The physician assured Havlicek that both Barnes and Mark Carlisle would soon be up and about.

"In fact," Trombley noted, "the sheriff was awake for a short time earlier this morning and asked for you. In a few days you should be able to talk with both of them."

Just before noon, Jed Hanes stopped by the doctor's office.

"The preacher at the Baptist church will perform the funeral service tomorrow morning at nine," said the deputy.

"Tell the preacher I'm grateful, Jed,"

"I'll be sure to do that."

After the deputy left, Cody ate a quick dinner and then spent most of the afternoon dozing. Returning to the Western Union office just before closing, he picked up the replies to his messages.

He read the telegrams, carefully folded the yellow flimsies, and slipped them into his shirt pocket.

"This just about wraps things up," he murmured in satisfaction. "A few questions tonight for Sloan and mebbe Yvonne Waters, and I'll have a pretty good case."

*   *   *

The funeral for Texas Ranger Hap Tompkins was short, simple, and well-attended. Most of the population of Alpine turned out for the service. The fallen Ranger's remains rested in a plain pine coffin at the front of the altar. His badge and a spray of wildflowers lay on the lid. Ranger Havlicek was asked to give the eulogy. His brief tribute to his departed comrade stirred most of the congregation.

"Hap, you were a good Ranger. When I was trapped on that same ledge where you died, I couldn't help but feel that you were there with me…not just your bones, but your spirit. I probably couldn't have stuck it out without your help. So, Hap, I'm gonna say thanks, and *vaya con Dios*."

At the end of the service, Hap Tompkins was laid to rest in the little cemetery at the edge of Alpine, with a roughly carved wooden cross at the head of his grave. Cody struggled mightily to keep his emotions in check as he shoveled the first clumps of earth onto Tompkins' coffin.

Once the burial was completed, Cody, along with the temporary deputies Jed Hanes and Deke Morris, headed for the Dust Devil Saloon. The members of the Alpine Town Council and Doctor Horace Trombley, acting mayor, attended the emergency town council meeting.

"Please, everyone, quiet so we can get started," Doctor Trombley shouted, thumping one of the saloon's bung starters on the bar. "Please, all of you, quiet! Once everyone settles down, Ranger Havlicek will explain about everything that's happened over the past few weeks."

Trombley hammered on the bar once again. The members of the council and the spectators took their seats; the babble of voices subsided.

"Thanks, Doc, or should I say Mayor?" Cody said as the room fell silent.

"I'm not much for speeches, so I'm gonna make this as short as possible," he explained. "As all of you are aware by now, Silas Dean has been arrested in connection with the murders of Texas Rangers Chance Lowney and Hap Tompkins, as well as the murders of Josiah Anders, Peter Hunt, Ted Boscobel, Paolo Alvarez, and Ross Moore. He's also facin' several other charges, includin' tryin' to finish me off."

"And that sure backfired on ol' Silas, didn't it?" someone yelled.

"Let Ranger Havlicek finish his story," Doctor Trombley ordered.

"Pete Sloan is also in custody for the same crimes," continued Cody. "He's willin' to testify against Dean, in hopes of avoidin' a hangrope. It'll be up to the court to decide Sloan's fate. I'll recommend, in exchange for his testimony, life in Huntsville."

"I still can't believe all this," said Stu Tate, one of the councilmen. "Why would Silas try and pull a darn fool stunt like that?"

"I'm about to explain," Cody answered. "Dean, along with Al Kroeger, had a scheme to take over this entire section of the state. Those hombres had eyes for all of southwest Texas. I suspect Dean might've even planned to run for governor eventually. Dean and Kroeger already bought up several businesses, usually workin' on the quiet by usin' an agent in Austin. They registered several of those purchases under false names to help cover their tracks. And, they had a couple other ways of gettin' their hands on an outfit if the owner didn't want to sell. That's where Miles Thibodeaux and Ned Riley came in."

"Dean and Kroeger were involved with those two?" Tate interrupted.

"They sure were," Cody confirmed. "Dean and Thibodeaux worked the same scheme back in Louisiana. Whenever Dean saw a business he wanted, Thibodeaux would get the owner in a poker game, or mebbe several games over a period of time. They'd play until the owner was in over his head. Then Dean would step in and buy the business cheap. Or lend the owner the cash to pay off Thibodeaux, then foreclose on him a few weeks later. Their plan worked until Thibodeaux killed a man over cheatin' at cards. Thibodeaux left Baton Rouge on the run, and Dean, knowin' he was finished in Louisiana, followed him."

Cody took a drink of water and went on with his story.

"They hooked up with Al Kroeger, who'd known Dean back in St. Louis. The three of 'em started the whole scheme over again. Kroeger put a twist to it by actin' as a law-abidin' newspaperman. It was Kroeger who brought in Ned Riley. If an hombre didn't want to sell out, and wasn't a gambler, then he'd call Riley in and have that person killed. Once the dead man's estate put the business up for sale, Dean would move in and buy it. That was one of his mistakes. He bought Moore's and Boscobel's stores in his own name."

Cody hesitated before he went on.

"Dean and Kroeger bought the Cross R as a headquarters for Riley and his bunch of renegades, usin' phony paperwork indicating the new owners were a syndicate from Chicago. I've got no way to prove this, but I'm positive Lem Tucker, the previous owner, wasn't killed in a fall from his horse. He was murdered for his ranch."

"But what put you onto Thibodeaux, Ranger?" Doc Trombley asked.

"A couple of things. First, he said he was leavin' Marathon and movin' to Alpine to avoid trouble. That didn't make any sense, with all the killin's up this way. Second, he never even came outside durin' that entire gunfight, nor afterwards, when everyone else in town had come out to see what had happened. That just didn't make sense. Why wouldn't he be curious about whether his pardners had managed to gun me down?

"I understand he made a real pretty speech just beforehand about not wantin' to fight the Texas Rangers, but that was only a blind. He was tryin' his best to keep his nose clean as far as the Rangers were concerned. Mostly though, it was just a gut feelin' I had. I really first got suspicious of Thibodeaux when I was playin' cards with him and three other men back in Marathon. The only player who lost big was Moe Levin, who owns the general store. That just didn't add up. So, I wired Cap'n Blawcyzk at Ranger Headquarters and asked him to check up on Thibodeaux.

"Sure enough, when the captain checked with Mississippi and Louisiana, he got the answers I expected. Levin would've been the next hombre to lose his business or die tryin' to hang onto it. Yvonne Waters confirmed that when I questioned her last night."

"But why did Thibodeaux and his woman try to kill you, Ranger?" asked Andy Millard, the blacksmith. "That doesn't make any sense. They could've just ridden out of town and gotten away."

"I was puzzled about that too," Cody agreed. "And like you said, at first look it doesn't make any sense. However, Thibodeaux had two problems. He didn't have any idea how much I knew about him. If Silas Dean talked, he'd have implicated the gambler. So, Thibodeaux figured he had to get rid of both of us. He was gonna kill me purposely with a gun so the noise'd bring everyone running. In the confusion, he'd head over to the jail and kill Dean and Sloan. He also probably figured he could get his hands on a chunk of Dean's money before he left town. Again, Yvonne Waters confirmed all this when I talked to her. Just like Sloan, she's willin' to testify against Dean. But you're absolutely right, Andy. If Thibodeaux and Waters had just left town, they would've gotten clean away. I still didn't have anythin' firm on either of them until after I heard from Austin. Luckily Thibodeaux made two mistakes, first by tryin' to kill me and second by not shootin' fast and straight enough."

Some members of the crowd snickered.

"Dean and Kroeger had the perfect covers as respected businessmen. If their plans had worked, they would have bought up most of the stores and freight lines around these parts, giving them a chokehold on the entire territory. You'd have been forced to pay whatever prices they demanded. Like Thibodeaux, though, they made one big mistake."

"They killed a Texas Ranger!" Stu Tate shouted.

"Two Texas Rangers, and nearly a third one, me," Cody reminded him.

"But their first real mistake was havin' Pete Hunt killed when he wouldn't sell out," Cody continued. "Unlike Boscobel, Ross, or Alvarez, Hunt's family kept pushin' to find out what really happened to him. They have plenty of influence at the Austin State Capitol, so they kept after the Governor until they got some action. Once Sheriff Carlisle asked for Ranger help, that cinched things as far as Austin was concerned. The Rangers started investigatin'."

"But how did those first two Rangers get spotted?" another of the councilmen asked.

"That's where Slade Hanscom came into the picture," Cody explained. "He was a clerk in the Adjutant General's office for quite a few years. He pretty much recognized just about any Ranger who rode down this way. Pete Sloan says Hanscom warned Ned Riley that Chance Lowney was on his way to Marathon to check out a lead he'd uncovered. Sloan also told me Hanscom had spotted Hap Tompkins as he was ridin' over Cross R range. Tompkins was caught, taken to Blue Canyon, and killed there. I'd imagine Deputy Ben Tate's body was also dumped into the canyon."

"But who shot Sheriff Carlisle and Joe Barnes?" Mike Hurley, from the Dust Devil, asked.

"As near as I can figure, Dean himself shot both of them," Cody answered. "Doc Trombley dug .41 caliber slugs out of Mark's back and Joe's chest. When I attempted to arrest Dean, he tried to plug me with a .41 caliber two shot Derringer. I'm still hopin' either Mark or Joe will be able to tell me for sure who shot them. But, I doubt if they saw anythin' but shadows. In one way, they were darn lucky. If Dean, or whoever plugged them, had been usin' a .44 or .45, neither one of 'em'd be around to talk at all."

Cody stopped to catch his breath.

"When I confronted Josiah Anders, the photographer, he was killed later that night. His shop was set ablaze to try and cover up the killin' and destroy any evidence. I managed to drag Anders outta the shop though, and before he died he told me about a steel box hidden under the floor. That box contained evidence which indicated Kroeger knew who had killed Ranger Lowney. In fact, who might have ordered it, and also information showing that Anders was blackmailing Kroeger and his pardner. Those papers are now safe at Ranger Headquarters.

"I couldn't figure out who Kroeger's pardner was until I was trapped in Blue Canyon. While I was thinkin' back over everythin' I learned since I got here, I recalled some legal notices I'd read in the Alpine Advisor. They showed Silas Dean had bought both Boscobel's feed store and Moore's harness shop. Once I got out of the canyon, I wanted to check the rest of the county land records, but Riley and his bunch didn't give me the chance. You know what happened when I rode back into town."

Cody paused again.

"Over the past couple of days, besides havin' Austin do that investigatin', I've gone over the county land records. You'll be able to hear all of the evidence once Dean and Sloan come to trial.

There's more than enough proof to send them both to the gallows. Yvonne Waters will probably spend several years behind bars too. It'll be up to the state's attorney whether or not to make a deal with Sloan, and up to a judge and jury to decide whether or not Silas Dean hangs."

Cody glanced at the clock hanging above the piano.

"And now, gentlemen, I've said all that I care to say. I propose a round of drinks on the house."

He grinned at Mike, the bartender.

"As long as those drinks ain't sarsaparilla!" Jed Hanes shouted and laughed. "Well, mebbe me and Deke'll make an exception, just this once."

20

After several more days of recuperation, Cody was strong enough to head home. Joe Barnes was back to work at his stable. Mark Carlisle, still in bandages and sling, resumed his duties as sheriff. Both of them were at Joe's livery barn as Cody readied Yankee for the long trip back to Austin. Cody saddled the big paint. The horse pranced, eager to travel after his days of confinement.

"Thanks again for everything." Sheriff Carlisle told Havlicek as they shook hands. "Silas Dean and Al Kroeger behind all this trouble…whoever would've guessed?"

The Brewster County sheriff shook his head in disbelief.

"Except a Texas Ranger," Joe Barnes broke in with a chuckle.

"I reckon you're right at that, Joe," Carlisle conceded. "Anyway Cody, if you ever get back down to this corner of Texas again, you be sure and look us up."

"You can count on that, Mark," Cody promised. "Besides, don't forget I've gotta come back to testify."

"I hope the only law enforcin' I have to do for the next five years is bustin' up ol' Tad Jones' and Cal Horton's arguments over their checker games," Carlisle chuckled. "And don't worry about me takin' it easy. I got word this mornin' that my wife's on her way back home. Gail'll keep me in line."

"She sure will," Joe Barnes laughed in agreement. "Cody, ask the sheriff about the time he told his wife he slept better in his bedroll when he was on the trail rather'n alongside her in his own bed. He had to sleep at the jail for a month after that one."

"You had to bring that up, didn't you, Joe?" Carlisle groaned.

"Of course, I did," Joe grinned. "Couldn't let the Ranger leave town without hearin' that story."

Cody laughed and turned to the hostler.

"Joe, I truly appreciate the care you've given Yank."

"Well, Cody, as much as I'd like to take the credit, most of that was Tommy's doing." Barnes admitted. "Your horse still don't like me all that much."

In punctuation to Joe's statement, Yankee flattened his ears and bared his teeth at the stableman.

"See what I mean?" Joe chuckled.

Cody swung stiffly into the saddle, wincing at a twinge of pain in his bandaged leg.

"You gonna be able to ride all the way to Austin with that leg?" Carlisle asked. "It's a long trip."

"I'll be fine once I loosen up," Cody replied.

Cody ran his gaze around the stable.

"Joe, speakin' of Tommy, where is he?"

"He was just around here somewhere," Joe answered.

The hostler cupped his hands to his mouth and called out.

"Tommy! Where you at, boy?"

Tommy finally shuffled in from the far back corral, his head hanging dejectedly as he dragged his feet in the dust.

"Yeah, Joe?" he asked.

"Cody's been lookin' for you. He's about ready to leave. Ain't you gonna tell him good-bye?"

Tommy lifted his head, his lower lip trembling.

"Where've you been, kid?" Cody growled. "And where the heck is your horse? She should've been saddled and ready to go by now. We're burnin' daylight, pardner, and I want to make Fort Stockton by tomorrow night."

"What do you mean, Cody?" Tommy exclaimed. "You're takin' me with you?"

"Would I have brought you this if I weren't?"

Cody leaned from his saddle to pick up a shiny new Winchester carbine propped against Brownie's stall.

"This is to replace your rifle that got shot out of my hand."

"This is mine?" Tommy asked, his eyes wide as Cody handed him the rifle.

"Yes! After all, we're pardners. Ain't we?"

Tommy nodded his head.

"I've got a Ranger pard by the name of Dade French," said Cody. "He got married awhile back to a fine lady named Sally, and they bought a little spread just down the road apiece from my ranch. I know for sure Dade could use a top hand like you once in a while."

Tommy stood frozen in place, not quite believing what he was hearing.

"And I've got a seven year old boy of my own. His name is Andy," Cody added. "He's got a baby sister named Abigail, but he'd sure admire to have a 'big brother' like you to pal around with. My wife Sarah's just about the best cook in all of Texas, too. 'Course, if you'd rather stay here, shovelin' horse manure all day long…"

"Not on your life, Ranger!"

Tommy dashed for his blanket and saddle. He lifted them from their pegs and tossed both on Brownie's back. He shouted over his shoulder.

"I quit, Joe!"

"That's gratitude for you," Joe laughed as he turned to Havlicek. "Ranger, you just made Tommy the happiest boy in the State of Texas."

"Seems like I lost my next deputy," Sheriff Carlisle chuckled. "It appears like the Texas Rangers'll be gettin' a good man in a few years."

Tommy led Brownie from her stall, slid the bit into her mouth, and climbed into his saddle. He leaned down to shake hands with Joe and Mark Carlisle.

"You be sure and keep that big ugly Ranger in line, Tommy," Mark laughed.

"Yeah, and if he gives you any trouble, you just let us know. We'll take care of him," Joe added.

"You can count on that," Tommy answered. "Good-bye, Sheriff. 'Bye, Joe."

"You about ready to ride, kid?" Cody asked.

Tommy lifted Brownie's reins.

"I'm ready, Cody," the boy grinned.

"Then let's ride, pardner. Mark, Joe, *Adios*!"

Side by side, Cody and Tommy galloped their horses out of Alpine, heading for home.

Notes

For those readers who may be unfamiliar with the expressions "pie-biter" and "biscuit-eater"—these are terms cowboys used to describe a horse that was spoiled by its rider, and hung around camp begging for treats.

To answer anyone who may question whether or not there truly is such an animal as a one-man horse, they do indeed exist, and many examples of them have come down to us through history. Nelson Lee, a Texas Ranger in the 1840s, owned a one-man horse known as the Black Prince.

One of the best-known examples of a one-man horse was an animal owned by a Prussian cavalry officer in the middle 19th century. Before the officer claimed him, this horse had killed several grooms by biting them in the abdomen. The horse was about to be destroyed until the officer entered his stall with a scalding leg of mutton hidden behind his back. When the horse lunged at his stomach, the officer quickly got the scalding mutton between himself and the horse, causing the horse to bite on the mutton and burn his mouth instead of biting his intended target. The horse never again tried to bite the officer, who took over his ownership. Some months later, in the midst of battle, the horse saved his rider's life by biting and ripping open the stomach of an enemy soldier who was about to run his sword through the officer.

Acknowledgements

I would like to acknowledge the following friends and experts, whose information and advice helped to make this book as accurate as possible within the realm of fiction. It was their assistance and dedication which made this work possible.

Texas Ranger Sergeant Jim Huggins of Company F, Waco, for his invaluable information on forensics.

The staff of the Texas Ranger Hall of Fame and Museum in Waco.

Karl Rehn and Penny Riggs of KR Training in Austin, Texas for their technical expertise on weapons of the period.

Deborah McConnell for taking the photographs of Yankee and me which were used by the publisher as models for the cover image, and Patricia Johnson for the author photo.

The Laudano family, owners of Twin Brook Stables in Clinton, Connecticut, for the outstanding care they have provided over the years for the real Sizzle and Yankee, and for allowing the use of their facilities for the photography session.

A special debt of gratitude goes to James Reasoner and his wife Livia (L.J. Washburn). Without their encouragement and guidance, I would never have begun this marvelous journey.

The "Owlhoot" Gang. You guys know who you are!

And finally, I acknowledge my many friends and coworkers at the Connecticut Motor Club. I won't attempt to list each one individually for fear of inadvertently missing someone, but I am extremely grateful to all of you for your support.